TIES THAT BIND

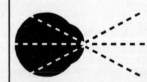

This Large Print Book carries the
Seal of Approval of N.A.V.H.

TIES THAT BIND

CHRISSIE LOVEDAY

THORNDIKE PRESS
A part of Gale, Cengage Learning

Detroit • New York • San Francisco • New Haven, Conn • Waterville, Maine • London

GALE
CENGAGE Learning·

LIBRARY OF CONGRESS CATALOGING-IN-PUBLICATION DATA

Loveday, Chrissie.
  Ties that bind / by Chrissie Loveday. — Large print ed.
    p. cm. — (Thorndike Press large print clean reads)
  ISBN-13: 978-1-4104-4802-6 (hardcover)
  ISBN-10: 1-4104-4802-9 (hardcover)
  [1. Large type books.] I. Title.
PR6112.O79T54 2012
823'.92—dc23   2012002842

Published in 2012 by arrangement with Chrissie de Rivaz.

TIES THAT BIND

CHAPTER 1

Sophie finished typing the last of the letters for the day and sighed. The end of yet another week of office temping. She hated the repetitive work, but needs must if she was to continue eating and add to her savings. This certainly wasn't the worst place to work but she had ambitions, plans which would not involve hours of typing.

She put the pile of letters and their envelopes together and took them to be signed. Everyone in the office was finishing off, clearing their desks and getting ready to adjourn to the wine bar next door for the usual Friday evening drinks.

After three weeks working in the same office, she had always been invited to join them but Sophie was becoming as bored with the routine as she was with the job.

"You are coming for a drink, aren't you?" asked Adam, the chief man in charge of IT systems.

"I was thinking of giving it a miss actually," she replied. "But thanks for asking."

"Oh, don't be like that. Come on. Or have you got a hot date?'

"Of course not." When did she ever have a hot date?

"Actually, there's something I wanted to ask you," Adam continued ominously.

Adam was the best-looking man in the office, according to a recent poll among the other girls. Trouble was, he seemed to have heard the news and she thought he was behaving like some superstar. Definitely not her type though he was certainly a look-twice or even three times sort of guy.

"I'll tell you later. Come on, everyone's beating us to the bar."

"Oh, all right. Why not?" It wasn't as if she had anything else to do, except maybe call at the local convenience store to buy something for supper. But she'd better stick to fruit juice.

Adam was attentive to her for most of the evening and she felt slightly self-conscious as the others were definitely noticing and nudging each other.

"So what's the mysterious something you want to ask me?" Sophie asked as the group was breaking up.

"Let's get something to eat and we can

talk about it then."

"I'm not sure . . ." She was distinctly cautious about getting close to anyone from a temporary post that was about to end.

"Come on. No strings, just a nice end to the working week. There's a good Italian a couple of doors down. My treat."

"Certainly not. We go halves, if I agree at all."

"We can argue about that later. So you'll come?" His startlingly blue eyes against his tanned skin and jet-black hair made an unusual combination. He was certainly good to look at but were his white teeth just a little too perfect? Who was she trying to convince? He was gorgeous. "Well?" he asked again.

"Okay then, thanks. But I'm paying my share."

"If you insist. Not sure why it matters so much but if that's the only condition, let's go."

"Night, Adam, night, Sophie. You in again next week?" called one of the other girls.

"I'm not sure yet. I've to wait for a call on Monday morning."

"Just behave yourself, Adam. Our Sophie may not know how to cope with you when you're on the rampage."

"I suspect Sophie is more than able to

look after herself," Adam retorted. "Besides, I'm a pussycat."

"Of the tiger variety, maybe!"

"Goodnight girls. Have a good weekend," he called after them. It was all very good-humoured but Sophie was beginning to feel slightly uncomfortable.

"Look Adam, I'm really not sure about this. What on earth do you want to say that had to wait so long, until everyone else had gone, in fact?"

"I wanted to ask a favour."

"And the favour is, exactly?" Sophie asked cagily.

"Let's go and eat. I'll tell you over a nice bottle of Chianti and some pasta."

Frowning slightly, she picked up her coat and followed him out of the wine bar. It was a warm evening and the pavements of the town were quite crowded. A few holiday-makers were beginning to arrive but it was still early in the Cornish holiday season. He held the door open for her and she sniffed appreciatively; garlic, olives, rich tomato and salad smells.

"I hadn't realised how hungry I am," she remarked.

It was crowded but they were shown to a small corner table.

"The tagliatelle is to die for. I'm going for

that with prawns," he announced, scarcely looking at the menu.

"If you recommend it, then I'll have the same. And you mentioned Chianti?" He nodded and gave the order to the waiter. "So what's all the mystery, and why me?" She leaned over to pick out an olive from the dish and nibbled it.

"I have to go to a wedding. A cousin of mine and I'm expected to spend the day with another frightful relative. I said I was taking an 'other' — but I don't have one."

"Another what?"

"You know, an 'and other'. I wondered if you'd be it?"

"No way! Especially not if it's tomorrow!"

"But I'm running out of options. Please say you'll help me out, Sophie. Please."

"So I suppose everyone else has turned you down?"

"Not at all, but it's a bit complicated. I did have a sort of girlfriend who I'd thought would come with me when I RSVP'd ages ago. But we broke up. I didn't even realise this blasted wedding was tomorrow until my mother phoned to remind me last night. I can't bear the thought of a whole day with Rachel."

"Sorry, it looks like you'll have to accompany her after all. She can't be that bad."

"Oh, she is. Please Sophie — save me! It might even be fun."

"How posh is it? I've nothing smart enough to wear to a wedding," Sophie said, close to relenting.

"Nothing special," he said with a pang of conscience. Most of the family were very well-off so it might be extremely smart. "Something quirky would be good, actually — make a statement."

"Right. Nothing special and something quirky? Actually, that probably describes my wardrobe exactly."

"Really? You always look so smart."

"Adam, the office wardrobe does not reflect my own choice of clothes." She laughed inwardly.

The office temping was simply to earn money. Her passion in life was clothes and fashion. One day her dream would be to have her own fashion business, but meanwhile, she had to content herself with building up her savings as much as she could. She delighted in trawling round charity shops and jumble sales. Period clothes and fabrics lent themselves to her style and many of them cost next to nothing.

"You must have something suitable to

wear," Adam was saying. "It'll be a nice meal, plenty to drink and at least some good company. Please say yes."

"Oh, all right. I've no plans other than washing and cleaning. But I'm still not sure why you're asking me. There are a dozen of us in the office and you probably know any one of them far better than you know me."

"Maybe that's the trouble . . . good; food at last. I'm starving."

The smell alone was enough to make Sophie glad she had agreed to join him for this meal. The green salad was dripping with a wonderfully tasty dressing and he had been right, the tagliatelle was to die for. They both remained silent for several minutes as they ate.

"So, you know most of the girls in the office — and that's why none of them would accompany you tomorrow? I'm the one that got the short straw, am I?"

"Not at all. Most of them are attached. Some of them are scarcely past being teenagers and I just don't fancy the rest."

"But you can't possibly fancy me. You hardly know me."

"You're smart, beautiful, competent, do the job well and don't ask me to fix your computer every five minutes. You're worth far more than being a temp."

13

"It pays the bills and I'm not stuck in the same office for ever. This is great food," she observed. "Can you pour me some more wine, please? Someone seems to have emptied my glass."

"I wonder who that was?" He laughed. "So, what do you like to do with your time if you don't commit to a full-time job?"

"Oh, this and that," Sophie answered somewhat evasively.

"Mystery woman, eh? As you like. Okay, so let's discuss tomorrow. The wedding is at noon, so I'll pick you up at eleven. Oh — depending on where you live? The wedding's at a National Trust House near Newquay."

"I live just outside Truro, in a rented a cottage on the Tregarth Estate," she replied.

"That's a drive of around forty minutes, so eleven should be fine, if that's okay with you. There's a meal at some point and the usual disco in the evening."

"Give me a clue about clothes," Sophie pleaded. "Something quirky may not be right."

"I don't know. I'm doing the dark suit, not morning dress."

"This could be a disaster in the making. Give me your mobile number, just in case I decide I can't do it."

He obliged and then scrawled down directions to her cottage on the table napkin.

"I really like you, Sophie and you don't seem the sort of girl who'd let a chap down."

"Let a chap down? How frightfully upper-class of you."

Adam looked away. He was probably a bit what she'd call upper-class. Public school, then university and now living rent free with his parents in a flat at their large house overlooking a creek near the South coast.

But what did all that matter? She was a bright lady, beautiful in every respect, perfect figure, naturally blonde (he was almost sure) with unexpectedly bright green eyes. He did wonder why she wasn't already with someone.

"Oh, I'm utterly posh, don't you know," he said with a ridiculously exaggerated accent. She laughed and swallowed the last of her wine as he added, "So, how about a pudding?"

"I think not. I'd better get going if I'm to find something stunning to wear tomorrow, in my extensive wardrobe."

She smiled. Her wardrobe was extensive — even if much of it was actually unwearable at the moment.

"Thanks for agreeing to come. I think it'll be fun. We can gossip about all my nefarious rellies and I can shock you with tales of their misdemeanours."

"Not too scandalous, I hope?" Sophie laughed with him.

"Totally," he replied with a shake of his head, as if it was too awful to contemplate.

"You're quite a case, aren't you? And yes, tomorrow might possibly be fun."

"And please, let me get the bill for this meal. As a thank you for agreeing to accompany me tonight as well as tomorrow. As I said, absolutely no strings attached."

"Okay then. Thanks. I'll forget I'm an independent woman for once. I'll pay you back by cooking a meal for you sometime."

"Sounds promising . . . so you don't hate me too much?"

"Payback could just mean I'm a lousy cook."

"Somehow I doubt that. I suspect most of what you do is always done to perfection. You interest me, Sophie James."

He paid the bill as they left and offered her a lift home.

"My car's parked near the market square, thanks. I don't merit a parking spot near the office.'

"I'll walk you there, then."

He put a friendly arm on her shoulder as they approached the car park.

"That's me." She clicked her key and the lights flashed on her little Smart Car.

"You can't be serious . . ." He stared at the tiny vehicle.

"See what I mean about me being quirky? It's a great little run-around-town car."

"Right, well, I'll see you tomorrow, then. And thanks for agreeing to be my 'other'."

"You have the directions safe?" Sophie asked and he patted his pocket. "You can always call if you get lost, and thanks for dinner, Adam — I enjoyed it."

As she drove back to her cottage, she thought of Adam and the prospects of the following day.

She had to admit that she was very attracted to the man. Who wouldn't be? But she was still scared of any sort of commitment, not that commitment was likely to become an issue in this case.

The last long-term man had turned out to be a disaster and she had been glad to escape unscathed except for a drastic loss of self confidence.

She was obviously a useless judge of character, and had decided to leave men alone for as long as it took.

Adam Gilbert. The office gossip suggested he always turned up to the office parties with different women and was therefore considered to be a bit of a Lothario.

He seemed nice enough, though, and she could surely cope for one day. He was obviously very bright and well educated. His technical expertise with computers and technology was apparent and, surprisingly, he showed great patience with the older staff who often struggled.

She looked forward to finding out more about him and perhaps his family too. It was a scary prospect in some ways but it was time she became more adventurous.

Besides, if she was ever to achieve her ambitions in fashion, this sounded like the sort of event that she could use to check out what people were wearing.

Despite feeling tired, she immediately delved into her various wardrobes to find something suitable for the following day. If it was taking place at a stately home, the wedding must be smart.

She picked up a silk jacket she had been working on recently. It wasn't quite finished but an hour or so of work, and it might be perfect. It was originally an old skirt she had cut up and pieced together, lined with a contrasting colour and stylish lapels of the same fabric. It was in shades of jade green, blending into blues with a flash of purple.

She had a long jade green skirt that went well with it. All good so far. Shoes and bag?

She foraged in one of the smaller cupboards and found a pair of high-heeled strappy sandals. The colour wasn't quite right.

Somewhere, she had a collection of shoe dyes that would surely contain something suitable. After a little more hore hunting and she found exactly what she wanted.

This was about to become a late night. It was almost one o'clock by the time Sophie had painted the dye on her sandals, completed the last bit of stitching on the jacket and finally pressed it.

"There," she said out loud to herself, satisfied with her evening's efforts. "My hoarding pays off like I always said it would. A complete wedding outfit in a couple of hours . . . except . . . I haven't got any sort of blouse to go under the jacket. It's okay without, but if it gets hot, I'm stuck."

She racked her brain for something suitable.

Somewhere, she was certain, there was a silk camisole top. She knew she wouldn't settle until she found it and began her hunt. Eventually, having remembered when she had last worn it, she discovered it in her dirty laundry basket.

With a sigh, she quickly rinsed it out and hung it up to dry in the bathroom.

"I hope it's all worth it, Adam Gilbert," she muttered as she fell into a deep sleep.

CHAPTER 2

Saturday began dull. Rain overnight had left everywhere damp and dreary-looking; not the best prospect for a wedding. Sophie looked again at her outfit and felt satisfied that it would do. It was all a bit of a gamble anyway, as she had no idea about the family she was about to meet. If Adam approved when he collected her, she would be happy. If he didn't, he could jolly well go on his own.

She made coffee and sat by the window watching the birds. It was such a lovely spot here. There were trees all around her and it was so well-sheltered that she got none of the rough winds that so much of Cornwall experienced.

She showered, washed her hair and brushed it until it shone before changing into her finery. She added a gold chain and packed a few necessities into the clutch bag she had chosen from her collection.

"Not bad, considering," she murmured to her reflection. She totted up the cost of her ensemble; well under twenty pounds and a few hours' work.

Adam's black sports car drew up outside promptly at eleven. He hooted and she went out, remembering to lock the door for once. Often she left it open, much to her parents' horror. But she had never considered being burgled in so remote a spot.

He stood beside the car with the door held open for her.

"Morning, Adam," she said. "I hope I'll do."

"You look stunning! Wow! I said quirky, but I never expected anything like this. I've only seen you in office suits before."

"I take it you approve." She laughed with relief, settling herself into the passenger seat.

"You'll do me proud."

"You look pretty good yourself — like the tie."

"One tries," he beamed as he pulled the car into the road.

They drove along the country lanes and a watery sun finally broke through.

"I'm glad it's clearing. It would be such a shame if the pictures were spoilt by rain. It's such a pretty house."

The row of cars parked outside made Sophie gulp. There were several top of the range models, a vintage Rolls Royce — which had obviously not even brought the bride! There was nothing else older than a year, in her estimation. There was money here, and a lot of it.

"Brace yourself. Here comes the maternal parent, desperate to see who I've brought. You okay?"

"I suppose . . . actually, no, I feel quite sick." Suddenly, in the face of all this apparent wealth, she felt conscious of her homemade jacket and dyed shoes. "I can't do this, Adam. You should have warned me they are all so well-off."

"Perhaps, but you can't back out now. You really do look stunning and I love the whole outfit. Confidence, girl, deep breath. My mother is all right really. Let her peer at you and she'll soon settle down."

"But looking around obviously, I should have worn a hat. Or at least one of those fascinators perched on top of my head."

"Certainly not — you'd have hidden your gorgeous hair."

He took her hand and gave it a squeeze. A smart, middle-aged woman immediately came over and took her hand. Her hat alone much have cost the high end of three figures.

"I'm Adam's mother. And you are . . . ?"

"Sophie James. How do you do?" she replied nervously.

"Morning, Mum," Adam said. "Sophie's a work colleague."

"I see. How long have you known each other?" she asked.

"Not long. Now can we cut the interrogation? Where's Dad?"

"He's talking to one of your uncles."

Mrs Gilbert spoke with an extremely refined accent and Sophie immediately felt out of place and out of her comfort zone. She smiled and felt reassured when Adam's hand rested beneath her elbow.

"You okay?" he whispered.

"Not really. You didn't say it was going to be such a . . . well, such a posh do. Everyone's so well-dressed and smart."

"As are you. You really stand out from the crowd. You look perfect and simply gorgeous. Now relax and try to enjoy it."

Sophie decided that she would cope if she considered it a research project and spent the time making mental notes of what colours people had put together in their outfits and what really suited whom. It calmed her nerves.

She looked forward to seeing the bridal gown. It was an area she really wanted to pursue. She had made a wedding dress for a friend, and it had been one of the most enjoyable things she had ever done.

"Lovely music, isn't it?" Adam whispered as they were seated and waiting for the service to begin.

"Er yes . . . I suppose so, yes . . . lovely."

At last the bride came in, and Sophie stared. She was much older than she had expected and the dress she wore was oh-so wrong for her shape and size. The fussy sleeves made the woman look top-heavy, and Sophie would have suggested a longer length and an elegant Empire line to slim her down.

"What's up?" Adam asked. "You look as if you're in pain."

"Sorry. I was just mentally re-designing her dress."

"She does look a bit meringue-like, doesn't she? Bet it cost a fortune too, knowing that family."

"Well, yes . . . hush now; they're beginning."

Adam spent most of the service looking at his companion. He'd picked her from the office group, knowing it would truly be a no-strings affair and anyway, he probably wouldn't see her after today. But he realised he didn't like that idea at all. She intrigued him. There was so much more to discover about her and, unexpectedly, he wanted to be the one to discover it.

She had a sense of fun he'd not noticed before and out of the standard office wear, her own style showed clearly.

He watched her eyes darting around the congregation, taking in . . . well, what, he wasn't sure.

At last the ceremony was over and the strident organ notes ushered the company outside for photographs.

"At least we don't have to pile into our cars and travel miles for the reception now," Adam said.

"Clever idea, licensing these places for the ceremony itself. It's all very picturesque and they do look very happy."

"I think they've been together for years, though I don't know why they suddenly decided to make it official. We'd better socialise, I guess, or my name will be mud with Mum. Don't worry, I won't leave your side. I suspect this photo-fest will go on for some time yet."

"Indeed, it always seems as if they have to take pictures of every possible combination of people," Sophie agreed. "But if you want to chat to people, I'll have a wander round the lovely garden. It's cleared up nicely and the sun is beginning to shine."

"Wandering round the garden with you sounds infinitely preferable to having pictures taken or chatting to anyone else. It's going to be a long day, so let's make the most of it."

Adam took Sophie's hand and, surprisingly, she didn't want to resist. It was hardly attaching strings, was it? Just a casual hand hold.

"So tell me about yourself, Sophie. What do you enjoy?"

"I quite like music. Most sorts really, but some modern genres leave me a bit cold. My parents are into ethnic stuff so I suppose I've grown up on a fairly eclectic mix. I love harmonies and guitar music."

"And what do you enjoy doing while you're listening to this eclectic music mix?"

"Well, sewing mostly . . . designing. I took a course in fashion design at university, although my parents insisted on an office computer course, too, so I could earn some sort of living if my dreams came to nothing."

"So you have dreams, then?" Adam smiled.

"Doesn't everyone? I'd really like to have my own design studio, or a fashion outlet. Some sort of business anyway."

"Fascinating." They had stopped walking and he was staring at her. "Did you know your eyes turn a much darker green when you show your enthusiasm?"

"What? Adam, aren't you even listening to me?"

"Of course I am. I was only commenting . . ."

"Well, don't. We have a no-strings agreement, remember?"

"You can't blame me; an innocent male, suddenly presented with the most stunning girl in the entire office, and I have you all to myself for a whole day . . . how am I expected to cope?"

"Don't be silly! We'd better get back to the party before you say something you'll regret," Sophie said with a peculiar mixture of embarrassment and excitement. "Stunning, did you say?"

"Certainly did! And I meant it, Sophie. Thank you so much for agreeing to come with me today."

"Thanks for the compliment . . . Come on, they must have finished snapping pictures by now."

She tried to sound casual but he still held her hand and she was beginning to feel slightly disconcerted. This whole thing was not going according to plan.

But she was actually quite liking the feeling. She dared not risk discovering she had feelings for Adam. She might never see him again after this weekend. No, she needed to keep tight control and simply make the most of her unexpected day out.

"Can you believe it? They're still snapping away, as you put it. Oh — this woman approaching with such intent is the distant cousin I was originally supposed to accompany. I do hope she's not going to cling to us," Adam whispered softly, leaning in close to Sophie before putting a wide smile on his face and calling out, "Rachel! Hi! This is Sophie, a close friend of mine . . . Sophie, this is Rachel . . . What are we — cousins nine times removed or something?" Sophie could see the effort Adam was making.

"Hello Sophie. Adam, darling." Rachel leaned over to him and gave him air kisses each side of his face, trying to grasp his hand and hold on to it. "Strange, I thought your current girlfriend was called something else. Or was that the previous one?"

"Jess and I finished a while ago. Sophie is a work colleague as well as a friend."

"Oh, I see. Just an office girl, then," Rachel purred.

Sophie squirmed and tried not to glare at

the woman.

"Actually, not for much longer," Adam said, much to her surprise. "She's starting her own fashion company soon. You need to watch out for her, she's going places, mark my words."

"That's certainly an unusual jacket," Rachel said, looking down the length of her nose. "Is that one of your designs?"

"Yes, it is, actually," Sophie said and Adam stared.

"You mean you actually made it yourself?" he exclaimed. "Wow — it's gorgeous! I assumed it was a designer label . . . someone else's label, I mean. Very stylish."

"I didn't realise people still made their own clothes," Rachel smirked. "How very economical of you."

"I prefer to think of it as ecological," Sophie retorted. "I believe in recycling fabrics and I intend to make a big thing of it when I open my shop."

Suddenly, her un-formed plans were crystallising. She would have a shop where she could work, make and sell her clothing, mostly to order. It would be a terrific gamble but she knew now it was what she wanted to do.

Rachel was smirking, hoping to discomfit the woman who looked like being her rival.

29

She and Adam were very distantly related, so much so that it didn't count, she had decided. He was good-looking and best of all, he was rich. She wanted him for herself.

"So your jacket had a previous life of its own, did it?" Her expression was distinctly sarcastic. "How fascinating."

"It did actually, if you must know. It was a silk skirt I picked up in a charity shop for next to nothing. The lining was once a shirt — silk too, of course — one has to be careful about mixing fibres." Sophie strove to keep her tone light.

"Goodness me." Rachel hooted with derisive laughter. "People will be fascinated when I tell them!"

"Excuse us, Rachel," Adam said. "We need to speak to some of the other guests."

He took Sophie's hand again and steered her away from the woman and her snide comments. "Ignore her," he told Sophie. "I am even more in awe of you. That jacket could have come off the racks in any of the big stores."

Sophie was still smarting from the verbal put-down. Pity, Rachel was a lovely-looking woman.

She pulled herself together. "You're showing a remarkable interest in fashion. I'd have thought a techie bloke like you would scarcely have noticed what women wear."

"Didn't I mention I have two older sisters? They've been making me look at clothes for most of my life."

"Sisters? Are they here today?"

"One's about to give birth and decided she couldn't face it. The other lives in the States and felt a remote family member's wedding didn't merit the expense of flying over. Not that she isn't rolling in dosh."

"It seems all of you are doing pretty well. I think it's time you shared your history with me. Lucky you, having two sisters. I'm an only child. Come on then, spill. Where do you live for a start?"

"I have a flat in town," he said evasively.

"So, where is it?"

"Rayman's Creek, if you know where that is."

"Wow — expensive area. A flat, though? I thought they were all massive houses down there?"

"Oh, dear." Adam sighed. "I suppose I have to admit my guilty secret. I still live at my parents' place. Shameful admission for a bloke of twenty-seven, I know . . . Well, almost twenty-eight, actually. You'd think I'd have moved out by now, but it's a nice place. Convenient for work and completely self-contained so I don't actually live with them, really, although Mum's always trying to feed me so it sometimes feels as if I'm still at home."

"If I had a lovely place like Rayman's Creek, I'd certainly want to stay there. So, what does your sister do in The States?"

"She runs the New York office," he said without thinking.

"The New York office?"

"Well, yes. Didn't you know we have a New York office?"

"You've lost me," she admitted.

"My father owns the company you've been working for. I thought you knew . . ."

"Oh, my goodness, I thought you were just the IT guy, not the heir apparent! I'm sorry Adam, I can't do this any more. I have to leave," Sophie flustered. "I'm totally out of my depth. I'll call a taxi. Make my excuses, please . . . say I was feeling unwell. I do feel sick, if I'm honest."

She almost ran away from the group and took the path towards the car park.

Adam called after her. "Sophie! Please, wait. Come back!"

How could he have done this to her? Sophie raged inside. Cosied her along to this blasted wedding where every single person was wearing clothes that probably cost more than she earned in a year!

There she was, sporting a homemade jacket cut out of someone's cast-off skirt, and dyed sandals. She was right out of her league. Adam's comments about her clothes were just a con . . . Oh, but those wonderful eyes of his hadn't looked mocking. It had been the awful Rachel who'd realised what she was — an impostor.

Sophie's brain was in total turmoil. She snatched at her mobile and clicked through the numbers to find her usual taxi company. She pressed the dial button and nothing happened. There was no signal.

Very well, she would walk to wherever there was a signal. Her silly strappy sandals were totally unsuitable for the terrain and it would be a long walk. It was deep in a valley and surrounded by trees.

She sat on the wall and gazed round at the array of posh cars. She'd bet at least one of them would have keys left in it and she could drive herself away and never see Adam or any of his relations again. It was tempting — but she blushed if she so much as made a private phone call from the office.

"What do you think you're doing?" Adam said as he finally caught up with her and plonked himself down beside her.

"Contemplating which car I should hotwire to drive away."

"I thought you wanted a taxi?"

"There's no phone signal here," she said with a shrug. "I'd walk if it weren't for these shoes."

"Indeed. Lovely though your shoes are, I agree, they're not suitable for walking. A perfect match for your skirt, though."

"Dyed."

"I see." His mouth twitched at the corners; he couldn't help it; he could contain himself no longer and laughed out loud.

Sophie glared at him. "How dare you laugh at me?" she retorted, trying to contain her anger by clenching her fists.

"I'm not laughing at you. I'm laughing because of this whole phoney gathering. Everyone pretending they're happy to be here and dressed to the nines just to make an impression," he told her. "And the one person who makes the biggest impact is ashamed of her talent! You, Sophie James, are the most remarkable person I've ever met."

He looked at her intently. "It wouldn't take more than a tiny smidge for me to fall in love with you, you know. You're refreshing, honest and sincere and I really want to get to know you. Please say I can attach just one tiny string to you?"

"You're an idiot!" Sophie scowled. "I'm not sure I can believe a single word you say. Besides, you hardly know me."

"Oh, but I do. I know you have dreams and ambitions — and I think I can help you to achieve them."

"I don't see how."

"Please come back with me now. Stop feeling so self-conscious. Forget Rachel's threats — she's just jealous. You probably have more talent in your little finger than all of these people put together. Most of them have been lucky to be born into wealthy families and have never achieved a thing."

"Aren't you one of them?"

"Not really. Okay, so I did go to a public school and I did go to one of the best universities, but I worked hard for it all."

He became serious. "My parents wouldn't let me have it easy. I'm just the IT guy, as you put it. I don't earn a fabulous salary because, although my father owns the company, he has a board and shareholders to answer to. He'd chuck me out along with anyone else if I didn't pull my weight."

He sighed, then went on in a lighter tone. "So, what do you say? Come back inside with me? There's smoked salmon and avo-cado mousse for starters."

"All right. But not just because I adore smoked salmon." She smiled but her eyes were serious when she added, "And Adam, I don't mind a small piece of string — just until we get to know each other a little better — but I reserve the right to keep hold of my scissors."

Unfortunately, they discovered they were seated at the same table as Rachel. Sophie drew in her breath in a heavy sigh, but felt Adam squeeze her hand reassuringly as she sat down.

"Everyone, this is my lovely girlfriend, Sophie James," he announced to the group. They murmured a greeting as a blushing Sophie smiled and nodded to them. "I'll let her discover everyone's names during the meal rather than bombard her with them all now."

His girlfriend? Since when did he think he could say that? Surprisingly, though, she found that she didn't really mind; even if it wasn't exactly true, it gave her a sort of status.

"Girlfriend?" Rachel snapped. "I thought you said she was just someone from your office who tagged along with you."

Adam glowered. Sophie was relieved that Adam's parents were at another table and hadn't heard these comments. Rachel was still glaring at her, clearly jealous that she had commandeered the man whom she had expected to be her escort for the day.

She was preparing something else to say to embarrass her rival, but tensions eased after the first glass of wine, and Sophie relaxed and even began to enjoy herself.

By the time the evening came and more guests began to arrive, the atmosphere changed. Sophie had met a large number of the family and, despite the awful wedding dress, she had discovered that the bride was a lovely lady.

"It's been lovely to meet you. Keep in touch, won't you?" she said as she left their table on her guest meeting circuit.

Even Mr and Mrs Gilbert seemed less formidable towards the end of the day. She had actually found Adam's father to be quite charming.

Dancing with Adam was a dream, especially during the slower numbers when he held her close.

But it wasn't long before Rachel came up to them. "My turn for a dance, Adam. She's commandeered you long enough."

"Sorry but we're about to leave," Adam replied. "I've ordered a taxi to get us home. I've had too much to drink to drive. I'll have to arrange a lift back tomorrow to collect my car."

"I can do that for you, darling," Rachel offered. "Or I could drive you home now."

"No need. Excuse us," Adam said firmly, guiding Sophie away from the woman.

"You might prefer to go back with your parents. I'm in the opposite direction to you," Sophie said.

"Not at all. It's not that far away. Besides, I'll get to enjoy a bit more of your company this way."

As it was, she fell asleep in the taxi, resting her head comfortably on Adam's shoulder. He woke her just before they reached her cottage.

"Wake up, sleepy head, you're home."

"I'm sorry. I wasn't much company after all."

"I enjoyed having you so close. I really like you, Sophie James." He walked her to the door and gently kissed her good night. "I want to see more of you, much more."

He kissed her again and the taxi driver gave a discreet honk of his horn.

"Well, how about I drive you over to collect your car tomorrow? It's the least I can do after such a lovely day."

"I accept, and gratefully. We could have lunch somewhere on the way back?"

"I seem to remember promising to cook you a meal. I could always stick something in the oven before I go, and it would be ready when we got back. Except that means you'd have to come here again tomorrow."

"No problem at all. Thank you very much."

"Thank you for asking me — and for persuading me not to give up and leave," she said softly, adding, "Goodnight, Adam."

"Goodnight. Sweet dreams. And don't worry about Rachel. She means nothing to me."

It was amazing how much could happen in twenty-four short hours, Sophie reflected. Her mind was full of a lovely dark-haired man with amazingly blue eyes. A man tall enough to rest his arm round her shoulders most comfortably.

And she was seeing him again tomorrow.

"Today," she reminded herself. "It's past midnight. Oh dear, I should have taken something out of the freezer for lunch," was her last waking thought.

CHAPTER 3

Sophie awoke to the ringing of her phone. She glanced at the clock as she answered it and saw it was way past nine.

"Hello? Adam?"

"Just calling to see how you are today."

"I'm not sure yet. I only just woke up."

"That's good; you haven't set off to collect me. Apparently my father also left his car at the wedding venue so he's called a taxi. I might as well go with him and come straight to your place afterwards — if that's good for you, of course?"

"Oh, right. I was going to have to call you anyway. You neglected to give me your address."

"So I did. I'll see you later. What colour wine should I bring?"

"Sorry?"

"What's for lunch? I don't want to commit the crime of bringing red wine if you're cooking fish."

"I suppose not. Definitely not fish, then. Probably something with chicken."

"That sounds good. I'll see you later, then — can't wait."

He rang off and Sophie lay back contemplating the coming day. She felt slightly nervous, cooking for the son of the boss of a large company. He must be used to dining in the best restaurants around the world, and here she was offering a piece of frozen chicken!

Crazy woman, she told herself. Doing the

exact opposite of what she had promised — no strings, she reminded herself.

Two hours later, she was adding another handful of fresh herbs to the casserole that was bubbling away gently. She was wearing jeans and a long, flowing shirt in a mixture of subtle shades that she had created from yet another of her charity shop purchases.

She laid the little table and picked the last few yellow and purple pansies from the hanging basket outside her back door. She had always loved the delicate little flowers, always thinking of them as tiny pieces of richly-coloured velvet patchwork — each one a work of art.

Before long she heard Adam's car coming along the track, and felt her heart thumping in a quite ridiculous way.

"Morning," Adam called as he slammed the door. "What a glorious day."

He came up the path and reached for her, pulled her into a long hug, ending with a kiss. She pulled back slightly, bemused by his greeting. Too much, she thought — even though she was loving every moment of it.

"Morning," she stammered. "Come on in. Or perhaps you'd prefer to be outside? Go for a walk?"

"Calm down. Sorry, I couldn't resist a

kiss, seeing you standing there looking so gorgeous."

"Adam, you're a lovely guy but please, let's take things a little more slowly. You're making too many assumptions."

"Okay, sorry again. I suppose I was but after yesterday, we seemed to be moving forward. So, a walk, then? Will lunch survive? I can smell something delicious cooking."

"It's in the slow cooker and I just have to cook the extra vegetables when we're ready."

He took her hand as they set off to walk along the path into the woods; she made no objection and they both relaxed and began to chat more easily. She pointed out a squirrel dashing up a tree and rabbits feasting on young grass in a clearing. He reacted as if he were seeing such things for the first time.

"You know, I never stop to look at things," he said. "I always seem to be in a hurry and for no real reason. Thank you, Sophie. I think you're going to be very good for me. Shall we go back now? I'm starving!"

"Do you realise how much time we've spent sitting over food since Friday?" she laughed.

"Eating is the most sociable way to get to know someone. It's great to relax over a meal, especially with some wine. Oh, that reminds me, I must get the bottle out of the car when we get back. I should have opened it before we left to let it breathe."

"Thanks. I do have some wine but I'm sure yours will be much better than the supermarket plonk I usually buy."

"Don't run it down. Supermarkets often buy their wine very well. This a lovely spot, isn't it? Very peaceful. But don't you ever feel scared, being so isolated?"

"Not really. Few people come this far off the track. The main visitor area is on the opposite side of woods. That's why this cottage isn't let to holidaymakers; it's too isolated for them."

He poured a glass of wine for each of them and watched as she moved around her tiny kitchen. He was fascinated by this woman and wasn't sure why. She was totally different from the usual girls he went out with, and half a million miles away from Jess, his last girlfriend. Sophie was so very refreshing.

"So tell me about your plans," Adam suggested. "How do you propose to work this business of yours?"

"I thought of a shop with a workroom. I'll make clothes on the premises, so it has to be somewhere that will attract customers or a place with parking where people can visit."

He frowned. "Sounds a bit impractical to me. You'd have to make a lot of sales to justify the rent, and you'd need a lot of stock ready to sell."

"I know. I have quite a collection already, and heaps of designs ready to be made to order."

"Why don't you sell from a website?"

"Eventually, maybe. It would work alongside the shop."

"I think you could consider the Internet as your main selling point. Get proper photos taken of your completed clothes and get a really good site created, showing designs for people to commission. You'd have virtually no costs and the only outlay would be the fabrics or whatever you needed to make things as they're ordered."

"Hmm, but I can't design a website. My computer skills are pretty basic," she admitted.

"But I can. I'd do it for you — then I can set you up with an account for payments and you're away."

"Wow, how exciting! I must say it all sounds amazing — and only slightly scary . . ."

"Have you got a computer?"

"Only an elderly laptop."

"I've got mine in the car. Let's see what we can do."

"Isn't this all a bit soon? I mean, you're rushing into this before thinking it through properly . . ."

"What's this — cold feet? Come on Sophie, this isn't the sort of ambition and drive I know you have deep down." Just then, his phone rang and he excused himself. She tried to guess who it was but his words gave nothing away.

"Look, understand once and for all, I am not interested," she overheard as he came back to the room.

"Sorry. Rachel again. I wish she'd stop plaguing me," he said sheepishly. "Now where were we?"

"Website? It's a totally different route to what I was planning but it makes sense, I suppose. If I can get it set up properly."

"I'm a professional, don't forget. So, what's your target market?" His enthusiasm was catching.

"Anyone really. I certainly don't want designs that only look good on stick-thin models, or outrageous things that no normal person could ever wear. I'd love to do wedding dresses, individually designed."

She became more animated as she went

on, "Like your cousin, for instance. I would have loved to have designed something that made her look elegant and that was right for her age. She's such a lovely lady, but she was the victim of some salesperson on commission. I realise there isn't enough money in wedding dresses alone, though."

"Well, let's see what's around, shall we? We'll have a search around the Internet. I'll just go and get my laptop."

"I'll put coffee on."

After all her years of dreaming and planning, it was scary to find someone was taking her seriously. Not only that, he was actually pushing her into it.

Was she ready? Certainly not. No more than she could allow this no-strings thing between her and Adam to progress.

She heard him coming back from his car and stopped staring out of the window.

"Right, now," Adam began, in a horribly businesslike way, "I suggest we look at . . . what shall we say, first? Wedding dresses? Get a feel for the sort of thing that's selling."

He typed the words and immediately thousands of sites came up. "Hmm. Looks like it's big business. What do you think of some of these prices?"

"Absolute bargains. I couldn't begin to

compete with that. That's depressing."

"But what you want to offer is something totally different. Personal designs. Okay, so we need to think round this. Can you actually make things here or do you need a proper workshop?"

"I usually work in the spare bedroom. It's quite large but there's not much room, though I manage."

"Show me."

She hesitated for a moment and then led him upstairs.

"It's a bit chaotic. I have loads of stuff stored and there are always several projects on the go at once."

He stood peering into the room and gave a small gasp.

"Chaotic is an understatement. Are all these your clothes?" He was staring at the long racks that stood the length of each side of the room, crowded with hanging garments. The work table in the middle almost filled the rest of the room. There was just room for an ironing board by the window and her sewing machine beside it.

"*My* clothes? Well, I own them, if that's what you mean. They're either completed conversions or essentially just materials waiting to be used. I never throw things away. That chest of drawers is full of trimmings, ribbons, binding, that sort of thing . . . threads, buttons, pieces of lace."

He was still staring — fascinated or shocked? She didn't know him well enough to determine.

"It's taken me years to assemble this collection. As my mother would tell you, I'm a born hoarder."

"Sophie, I don't know what to say. I've never seen anything like this. To think, that smart lady in her neat suit at the office has all this behind her?"

"And who would have guessed that the smart IT bloke in the office is really the heir apparent to the whole business, with offices overseas into the bargain?"

"I think that coffee may be ready," he said with a grin. "You're amazing Sophie James." He caught her as she passed him in the doorway and pulled her close to him. He kissed her gently and smiled down at her, lifting her chin to look into her eyes. "I suspect those strings might be becoming more attached."

"Please, Adam. Don't get all serious. I'm not in the market for any sort of attachment."

"Well I hope you don't take too long to decide you are. Come on then; coffee, if you insist." His phone rang again. He cursed as he answered it.

"Where I am is irrelevant. I've told you, I'm not interested. Goodbye." Angrily, he switched the phone off. "I'm at a loss to know how to get rid of Rachel."

Sophie smiled as they went downstairs — but not before she caught him giving a lingering look towards her bedroom.

His kiss had been very tempting, though, and held a promise she'd thought she would never know again. It was all rather sudden and somewhat disconcerting.

Quickly, she led the way down.

"I think what you're offering is unusual and a fairly specific market," he told her.

"I know," she said, a little downhearted. "I'm so afraid that Cornwall isn't the right area but I couldn't bear to move away. I've lived here most of my life and I love it. I need to be near the sea and this is such a wonderfully secluded place. How do I find a market in such a remote corner of Britain?"

"That's where the Internet comes in. It's a global market and anyone can access it from everywhere. But initially we need to get your name out there — perhaps a fashion show launch?"

"What? A fashion show? Me? I'm not yet ready for that. I wouldn't have the nerve.

And suppose nobody came?"

"Make it an event for charity," he suggested. "Choose the right one and they'll seize the chance to sell merchandising which will also give us some publicity."

"But where would we hold it, and how do I get everything ready in time?" Sophie's eyes were wide with alarm.

"Sophie . . . You can do it. I'll help you all the way."

"But I'll need models . . ."

"The girls in the office would be delighted to be models, and they come in all shapes and sizes, just like you wanted. We can get giant pictures printed and mounted to show off the other designs that you can make to order, as well as lots of drawings of your wedding dress ideas."

"Oh, Adam, you make it sound so easy. Why are you supporting me like this?"

"Because I care, Sophie. I want you to succeed and show the likes of Rachel that people don't have to be born rich to make things work. I was so proud of you when she was bitchy to you yesterday; you rose above it and proved you were a hundred times better than her." He smiled warmly at her.

"Well, thank you, Adam. I thought . . . well I did feel a bit foolish, in my homemade jacket and all."

"Like I said at the time, I could hardly believe it was home-made; it was very professional, not at all amateurish."

Sophie felt herself blushing and tried to cover her confusion by pouring more coffee.

"Thanks," he said. "Now, what do you call yourself?"

"What do you mean? Sophie James, of course."

"Okay. It's a nice enough name, but does it have the sort of ring to it that one needs in the fashion world?"

"I haven't thought about it, really."

"If we come up with something better, we can change it."

For the next couple of hours, Adam worked on creating her sales pitch on his laptop. It was certainly a lovely machine and made hers look almost like an antique. She was fascinated watching the speed and expertise with which he was working.

"Right," he said at last. That's the basics sorted and stored on my machine. Now we need to decide which clothes to photograph and put on the website. I think your jacket could be one of them."

"It's not for sale, though."

"It doesn't matter, it's still a good advert

and a fine example of your work. We can always label it as sold. Shall we go and look through what you have?"

"Adam, I'm so grateful to you for doing all this but it's already nearly eight o'clock. Don't you have to be somewhere?"

"Not really. I am getting a bit peckish, though. That was a lovely lunch but it was a long time ago."

"I could do cheese and salad sandwiches, if that's okay?"

"That sounds perfect, thanks," Adam said, beaming at her.

Still feeling bemused by the speed at which things were happening, Sophie sliced tomatoes, wondering how all this could be happening to her. If she wasn't careful she could be sinking in much too deeply — on all counts.

Fashion shows, websites, giant blown-up pictures of her designs . . . it all sounded like a recipe for disaster or something so wildly expensive that her meagre savings would disappear in a flash. One thing she would not do was get into debt, and nor would she allow Adam to fund anything for her.

"That looks great to a starving man," he said when she brought a tray laden with sandwiches.

"I've made some tea as well," she told him. "Knowing you have to drive, I thought more wine wasn't a good idea."

"You're probably right. Though I could always find an alternative to driving home . . ."

"Adam," she chided. "What did we agree about strings?"

"If you insist. It was just a thought. But the more we work together, the harder it'll be keeping those strings under control."

"You'll be back in the office tomorrow," she reminded him. "And I'll be here in my own little world."

"I could always suggest you're needed in the office."

"Actually, I could do with a couple of days to think about your suggestions. I need to go through my clothes to see what's really possible for a show and for photography."

"All right, as you like. But if it's okay with you, I'll come over tomorrow night and we can talk some more. I do actually feel quite tired now, so it's probably as well to call it a day. I'm really excited by all of this. I think it's going to be a good plan and 'Sophie James Fashions' could be the next big thing. I think we need to find a better name, though — one that will reflect your eco-friendly elements as well, perhaps."

"You're amazing. You just hear an idea and suddenly, you're planning a whole future for me."

"I thought I might run it past my sister in New York. She's the really trendy one in my family. Would that be all right with you?"

"It's a bit scary. But everything is a bit scary, so do what you think is right. But please realise that my funds are extremely limited. I've been saving hard whenever I can but it still doesn't amount to much. Hiring premises, printing giant posters and putting on a fashion show with the sort of glitz that needs to go with it, sounds way beyond my means."

"We'll talk it through tomorrow. I have some contacts I can speak to for discounts and printing's no problem since I can get it done through the company. I work hard enough for them, they can afford to do me a favour or two. As for glitz, it's easy to make something look glitzy without spending a fortune."

"Okay. Tomorrow night it is, then."

"How about eating at your local pub; then we can come back here after a quick supper and take stock?"

"Sounds good to me." Sophie couldn't help smiling.

"Admit — you're as excited as I am."

"Okay, yes, but a bit scared, too — scared but excited."

"Good. I am too. I'm already seeing myself as a fashion entrepreneur. My sisters will be so impressed. They'll want to know what sort of goddess could possibly have inspired me!"

"Gosh, I've never been called that before! Goddess of the earth, that's me!" Sophie laughed to cover her embarrassment.

"That's Gaia, isn't it?"

"I think you're right . . . oh, wait! Fashions that reflect caring for the earth? How about Gaia Fashions?"

"That's a good start; we'll work on it. Now, if I've really got to go home, I suppose I'd better go."

"We were late last night and I was late the night before. No way could I be in the office at eight-thirty in the morning."

"And if you get a call tomorrow?"

"I'll sleep through it!" She showed Adam to the door.

"Goodnight, Sophie." He pulled her close and shared another kiss with her. When she felt herself almost trembling, she pulled away, afraid of allowing herself to weaken and let the strings spin a web round her and envelop her completely.

As she lay in bed, she thought of all that had been happening. Adam was certainly a force to be reckoned with. He'd got the bit between his teeth and was galloping away with her ideas. It was exciting, all right — *he* was exciting — but was it getting beyond her control? Surely she had been thinking about it long enough, she told herself. Now it was time to act on her dreams.

CHAPTER 4

Sleep was a long time coming for Sophie. Meeting Adam was the highlight of her life so far, and merely thinking of him was keeping her awake. But he was so very different to her; his background was one of wealth and privilege, even if he did work hard for a living.

Her own parents were lovely, hard-working people who never had anything come to them easily. She suspected there was a lot more to their one-time hippy lifestyle than they would ever admit, but they'd always enjoyed life and were devoted to each other. They'd married young, but were well into their thirties before she was born. Their motto had always been "work hard and you'll get on in life".

How could she ever move into Adam's sort of world? She was ill-prepared for that kind of life, should it ever come to that. It would be all too easy to fall in love with him and become another in his trail of broken hearts.

No, she must keep their relationship on a businesslike level. If they were going to work together on her fashion project, they had to find a way to work without emotional involvement.

Despite feeling weary, she rose early and hoped she wasn't called to some new job. She hated turning work down, but on this occasion, she had loads to do and think about.

Sorting through some of her stock was a priority; any clothing that was complete should be put on one rail and things that were nearly finished had to be sorted and finished.

Then she needed to look at her portfolio of designs and work on them.

She needed a list . . . several lists. If Adam was coming to help her with a stocktake of sorts, she had to be at least slightly orga-nised. The time for playing with ideas was over and hard work and decisions were the next tasks.

By the end of the afternoon, she was grubby, weary and even more confused. She slumped down with a cup of hot chocolate and realised that she was a total mess.

Her mind was a mass of unformed ideas. She'd never had any organisation, making clothes out of recycled materials with no thought given to sizes. She had worked on impulse and taken inspiration from the fabric itself without proper motivation.

"How can you possibly think of turning this stupid hobby into a proper business?" she wailed at nobody.

Adam would be here in half an hour and she needed a shower and to change into something that a prospective fashion designer might wear.

On the other hand, they were only going to the local pub for a bar snack rather than somewhere for a posh meal.

She was just drying herself when she heard a car stop and seconds later someone at the door. She leaned over the banister and yelled for him to come in.

"Sorry, I'm running late," she called down.

"Need me to come up and dry your back?" Adam called up cheekily. "You assumed it was me at the door. Was that wise?"

"No one else ever comes out this far. Anyway, I heard your car stop and recognised the sound of the engine," she fibbed.

"Really? I'm impressed. Well, hurry up and we'll go and eat."

Instead of a carefully planned outfit, Sophie flung on some jeans and a casual shirt and ran down the stairs.

"Sorry, I lost track of time," she said.

"No problem. I was a bit early. It's good to see you; I missed you being around the office." He reached over and drew her close to him. He kissed her but she pulled back, remembering her decision of the previous restless night.

"Adam, we can't . . . I mean we mustn't . . . oh, I don't know what I mean," she said, frowning. "I can't get too close to you, not when we have to work together. I won't let myself become another victim in your trail of broken hearts. My future means too much to me. So, if you don't mind . . ."

His face took on an anguished expression; he looked quite crestfallen and those devastating blue eyes seemed to cloud.

"I'm not sure what I've done to upset you," he murmured. "I thought things were going well between us. Is there something wrong? I mean, has something happened since last night?"

"Not really, I've just had time to think, that's all. Your world is so different from mine. I've always had to work hard to get what I wanted. I'm sure you work hard too, but you don't realise what all this means to me."

"I do care, Sophie, really I do. I'm amazed at your talent and your ambition and I was hoping we might eventually have a future together. I don't know what you've heard to give you the idea that I leave trails of broken hearts, but I assure you I'm not like that at all."

"Perhaps I misjudged you, but when you won the 'best-looking man in the office' vote, the girls said you brought a different female to every party."

"Could we rewind, please? What vote was that?"

"Sorry. Shouldn't have mentioned it." She couldn't help a grin spreading over her face.

"Come on. I need to know what's been going on."

"The girls all voted for the best-looking man in the office and you won. Don't get carried away — it's only those blue eyes of yours that won it."

"Hmm, I'm flattered anyway . . . best-looking, eh?"

"Leave it off. I'm still concerned about this trail of women."

"I only took Jess to one party. Think I missed most of the rest . . . oh no, Marnie did come over for one . . . my sister Marnie, that is, from New York."

"Okay, maybe they were exaggerating. All the same, while we're working together, let's keep it business — no strings, remember? I'm nervous enough about all the plans anyway. I don't need any more complications."

"What a pity. I was getting slightly addicted to kissing you. Maybe the occasional kiss could be allowed?"

"Well . . . maybe . . . But I have to keep those scissors handy to cut the strings if they get too tight."

"In that case, shall we go and eat now? I'm starving."

"Fine. Though I can see myself putting on pounds if we spend most of our time together eating. Do you work out?"

"I swim most mornings, in the pool at home. Do you like swimming? You must come over and use it sometime."

"I'd love to, thanks. I'm not a good swimmer but I do enjoy it. Wouldn't your parents mind?"

"Of course not, why would they? I can invite whoever I like. I'm a big boy now."

They went out to his car and looked up, startled, as a strange car suddenly drove away at speed.

"That's funny," Sophie said. "Nobody drives down this track unless they're coming to see me; it doesn't go anywhere else."

"Someone lost, perhaps?" Adam suggested. "It looked a bit familiar, but I suppose sports cars are fairly common. Make sure you lock your door, though, just in case."

They drove to the little pub, neither of them noticing the car that was now parked among the trees.

It was a pleasant meal; nothing dramatic, just well-cooked, plain food. Adam insisted on paying and Sophie protested.

"You can always cook for me again," he told her with a grin. "Besides, your living expenses are more than mine and you're not earning at present. When you're a top designer earning pots of money, you can pay for me then."

"Deal," she agreed. Over their meal, she had brought him up to date on her day's work. "So you see, I do have a huge amount of work ahead."

"In that case, keep your phone switched off each morning in case anyone calls you in to work. I've made heaps of progress too. I contacted various people I know and we can do the fashion show quite soon. It's March now, so I'd suggest May or early June. It needs to be well before the main holiday season starts so we can get a hotel booked. I was thinking of the Hall for Cornwall in Truro but that may be a bit ambitious."

"Adam!" she sqeaked. "The Hall for Cornwall is huge, not to mention very expensive to hire. I was thinking more along the lines of some village hall; something modest, for a start."

"It needs to be a decent venue with comfortable seats and a nice atmosphere, but we can thrash that out later. We need to decide on other things first. Let's get back to your place and I'll have a look at what you've been doing today."

Sophie was silent as they drove back.

Clearly Adam was on a totally different planet. Hall for Cornwall, indeed! It was the major concert and theatre venue in Cornwall and about a million miles away from her own thoughts. How on earth was she going to manage to produce anything like a decent fashion collection in time?

Her stock was little more than a pathetic little group of clothes that appealed to her and her work ethic of recycling fabrics. She wondered how Adam could possibly have such utter faith in her work.

"Why, Adam?" she asked out loud.

"Why what?"

"Why do you believe in me when you hardly know me?"

"I don't know. I'm just convinced you can make your dreams come true with a push or two in the right direction."

"Well thanks for the vote of confidence but I still think you're being very optimistic — especially since this is all on the strength of one jacket isn't it?"

"And the shining light of ambition in your eyes when you were talking about it. I emailed my sister, by the way. She wants to see pictures and hear all about it. She said she'll come over for the show, too."

"You're mad, Adam Gilbert. We've not even got a show yet and you're inviting people over from America?"

"Incentives, my dear Sophie. Here we are. Let's see what you've been doing all day."

She felt nervous. He was showing such confidence and she felt as if there was very little to show for her efforts. What on earth could he be expecting?

"I'm looking forward to seeing your design drawings."

"I hope I don't disappoint you."

"You really do need your confidence, don't you?"

"I've never shown anyone these things before, it's a bit like showing your essay to a teacher at school."

"Don't worry, I'm not going to be giving you marks out of ten."

"I've got a long haul ahead of me to complete a collection."

"How long can you manage without earning money? I mean, do you have to go out to work or can you work on the collection?"

"Well, without delving too deeply into my savings, I'm good for a few weeks at most. My main savings pot I want to use to buy fabrics and have something to spend on the show. I can't use entirely second-hand fabrics, not for the new designs."

"So, ideally, you need the odd order or two to bring in some income before the show. That way you'd have some money and possibly a garment or two to use?"

"Sounds a bit hopeful. What did you have in mind?"

"I have yet another cousin who's getting married in a few weeks, well about three weeks, I think . . . now this is Marnie's idea . . . if you could design and make her wedding dress in the time, she might let you use it in the show as a sort of special presentation. The show-stopping finale."

"Wow, that would be terrific! Do you think there's a chance she'd buy such an important dress from an unknown designer?"

"If I sell it right, she will — and you can come up with something spectacular."

"Oh, Adam, that would be amazing. When can I meet her?"

"Steady on. I have to do a sales pitch first. Let me look at some of your stuff."

He laughed out loud. "Oh, Sophie, that's why I think we can do this. You should see your face — it lights up when you're enthusiastic." He opened his arms and pulled her close.

He was just too good to resist and she allowed herself to be kissed yet again.

"Oh, dear," she whispered. "This is all going to be very difficult. I have to get some willpower from somewhere."

"Shouldn't bother, if I were you," he murmured. "I'll only try to demolish it again right away."

"You're so bad for me — in the nicest way — but this is not getting us anywhere."

"Oh, don't know about that . . ." he said

with a wry grin.

"Adam!" she said firmly. "We need to concentrate. Come on, look at these sketches."

He picked up her large folder and turned over the pages. He looked and said nothing. He went back to the beginning and looked again. She watched his face, searching for a sign of like or hate but he remained impassive. She could wait no longer.

"You hate them, don't you? I'm no good. You should just forget about me and I'll potter on forever, making stuff I can never wear."

He stared at her and she turned away.

"Sophie, please shut up. I don't think they're rubbish at all. In fact, some of these are spectacular. Some of the colours I don't like, but the shapes are good; clean lines and interesting features. You really have got something."

He looked over her shoulder. "Have you got some wedding dress designs?"

"In another folder. Hang on." She rummaged beneath one of the clothes racks and pulled out another artwork folio. "There you go." She laid it on the work table and left him to look through it. Again he remained silent until he had gone through it twice. She was almost biting her nails by the time he looked up.

"That was a million times worse than waiting for the teacher to read an essay," she said nervously.

"I think they're amazing."

"Now you're being sarcastic."

"I'm not being anything but honest. I love them. Have you made any of them yet?"

"Well, no, there's not much point making anything like this unless it's commissioned. The fabric's far too expensive and anyway it's important to get the right fit." She bit her bottom lip. "So, do you really think that your cousin might choose a design from me?"

"If you can make it quickly enough. The wedding's been arranged in a hurry as they're moving overseas and want to marry before they leave."

"No problem. Always assuming she'll like what I show her."

"I'll arrange for her to meet you, then. Show me what else you've got. Those look finished, on that rack." He pointed.

For the next hour, they pulled things around and held up garments until at last they reached the end of the rail of clothes and Sophie said, "You seem to know an awful lot about clothes."

"For a bloke, you mean?" he teased.

"Well, yes, I suppose so. It seems a long way from your actual job and presumably your interests."

"I have two older sisters who were always watching anything on television to do with clothes. Marnie is particularly interested in fashion. Bee used to be before babies took over her life, but they both spent hours looking and buying. I got dragged along and was expected to make proper comments about what suited them and what didn't. I do actually find it quite interesting — from a sort of construction perspective, I suppose."

"I see. So maybe you are a good critic, after all, and I should make use of your honest opinions."

"I hope so. As long as you promise that if I give honest criticism it won't spoil our relationship."

"As long as it's constructive criticism and truly honest."

"So, how long would it take to make a wedding dress?"

"That depends on the style and fabric. If I work exclusively, probably four or five days could do it. For a simple style, less. Don't forget, starting with new fabric is much quicker than unpicking and re-working old fabric."

"So how do you know what to buy, how much fabric do you need?" he asked.

"Just practice. I don't like to buy too much and then have to waste it, but I have to allow for a bit of variation, of course."

"I think you're a genius. I'll fix up a meet with Chloe and then it's up to you. I know you won't let me down!"

She watched him drive away. It worried her that she felt a degree of reluctance to see him go. Something continued to nag at her. Her last relationship had ended when she had felt manipulated all the time. He had always wanted to be in charge and tell her what to do. Wasn't Adam beginning to do the same thing? But the trouble was, this time she was rather liking it.

She went into the kitchen to make a hot drink and immediately noticed broken glass scattered all over the sink. She pulled back the curtain — the window had been smashed! Fortunately perhaps, the window was too small for anyone to have climbed in, but it was disconcerting to think that someone had broken it deliberately. She stuck some thick card over it, knowing it would have to be replaced sooner rather than later. How on earth could it have happened?

CHAPTER 5

By ten o'clock the following morning, Sophie had arranged a meeting with the bride-to-be; Adam had wasted no time in calling his cousin and she had then phoned Sophie. The broken window would have to wait.

They arranged to meet later, in a coffee bar in Truro so that they could then go and look at a large fabric shop in the town. Her excitement stopped her from feeling worried about the broken window.

Clutching her folder of designs and several sheets of plain paper, she arrived early at the meeting place. Chloe bustled in minutes later, full of apologies.

"Sorry, life is manic at the moment. I can't believe how much there is to organise!"

"Lovely to meet you, and thank you for giving me the chance to show you some designs. I've ordered coffees."

"Adam sold you well, said you are brilliant and that you could make whatever I want. You do know there isn't much time?" Chloe said. "My fiancé's appointment in New York was only confirmed last week and we decided to get married before we go. It makes the visas simpler if we're a married couple."

"No problem for me. Did Adam tell you the rest of the plans? About the fashion show?"

"Yes, he did. I felt sad I won't be here to see it. He also said you might like to use my dress in the show?"

Sophie flushed. "That was presumptuous of him."

"Typical of Adam, though. But it's no problem, since I'd have left it behind anyway." She laughed. "I don't plan to have a second wedding any time soon."

"Always assuming you want to buy it from me, of course."

"I'm sure I will. I haven't seen anything available that I could see myself wearing. Do you have something for me to look at?"

Sophie passed a small portfolio across the table. "These are just rough ideas. Some of these are certainly not right for you, now that I've met you, but I'd design and make exactly what you want and it would be exclusive."

"Exclusive sounds expensive . . . I do have a budget . . ." She named a figure that almost made Sophie gasp. Though she knew the family were wealthy, she hadn't expected such a generous figure. Maybe she needed to fix prices more sensibly and not be thinking of economies all the time.

"I know I can produce something stunning for that kind of budget. Shall we get down to business?"

An hour and three cups of coffee later, they had the style finalised. Sophie made some quick sketches as Chloe spoke and she was delighted with the results.

When they went to the fabric shop, Sophie was in her own particular paradise. She fingered through various fabrics and selected a few that would be suitable. She asked for samples of Chloe's favourites and stored them carefully in her bag.

"The next move is a fitting session. I'll make up something in muslin to establish your exact size and shape and then we'll decide on the fabric. Can you come to my cottage tomorrow?"

"That soon?" Chloe asked in amazement.

"We need to make sure it's all done in good time, so the sooner we start, the better."

"That's great," Chloe agreed. "I can't thank you enough for taking this on, Sophie." She lowered her voice when she added, "Tell me, are you and Adam . . . well, you know . . . an item?"

"Not really. We only met last week at someone's wedding. Well, longer I suppose, as I was working in the office as a temp."

"He seemed pretty smitten." Chloe smiled. "And I can see why. It would be good to see him settled, he's a lovely bloke."

"I'm sure he is, but he's just making it all happen so quickly. It's only been a few days and here I am with a commission for a wedding dress, and a fashion show in the pipeline."

"That's typical of Adam — never did let the dust gather! And I love your work, too. But I must be off — I've a million things to do. Thank you so much, Sophie. See you tomorrow."

Chloe kissed Sophie on both cheeks and rushed away.

Sophie went back into the fabric shop and bought several metres of muslin to make the base model. She also had a busy evening ahead of her.

Her phone rang as she was driving back, but she had to leave it until she stopped. It was a missed call from Adam, but he hadn't left a message. She hesitated, but decided not to call back. She needed to begin her work and went straight up to her workroom.

A short time later, she heard a car stop.

"You there, Sophie?" Adam called out. "You left your door open again. I could be an axe murderer!"

"Hope not," Sophie laughed. "I'm too busy!"

"How did the meeting with Chloe go?"

"Fine. She's pretty well committed. I have to make up the base model tonight since she's coming here tomorrow for a proper fitting and to decide on the final style and fabric."

"Wow, that's great — well done! Did you talk money?"

"Vaguely. I just hope I'm worth what she suggested was her budget." Sophie felt herself flush a little.

"First rule. Don't underprice yourself," Adam said cheerfully.

"But I'm only just starting out," she countered.

"Precisely. You have to make sure you charge what you're worth right from the get-go. Now, have you eaten yet?"

"No and I haven't got time to."

"Never fear — I have supplies in the car so I'll go and cook something for us both."

"Oh, I couldn't, Adam — you've already done enough."

"I intend to stay around for the evening so let me do my thing." He turned towards the door. "And I can ply you with coffee to keep you awake if necessary," he called as he rushed down the stairs. She heard noises from the kitchen and gave a shrug. Let him get on with it.

"What happened to your window?" he called from the kitchen.

"It got broken and I haven't had time to get it fixed."

"But how did it get broken?" he asked, coming back upstairs.

"It was like that when I got in last night."

"Have you reported it to the police yet, Sophie?"

"Of course not. Who's to say it was done deliberately?"

"That car we saw last night. I wonder if that had anything to do with it?" Adam looked concerned but went on, "Have you got a corkscrew hidden somewhere?"

"Second drawer on the left," she replied. "But I shouldn't drink much. It's going to be a long night."

"I need some wine for cooking," he answered and went downstairs again, leaving her to it.

Sophie laid out the muslin and began to cut a rough base shape for the dress to make up and tack it together for fitting. It was easier to adjust the fit and then use the muslin pieces as a pattern for the actual fabric.

Smells of something delicious began to

waft up the stairs and her tummy rumbled. In her excitement, she realised she'd forgotten to eat any lunch. Suddenly, interest in her design and the wretched muslin waned, food became a priority and she trotted down the stairs.

"You wretch!" she laughed. "Employing distraction techniques on a poor, starving seamstress. What are you making? It smells divine."

"Only a stir-fry — highly nutritious to keep you working through the night. Good news though, isn't it?"

"It's great. Thank you so much. I really liked Chloe," Sophie said. "She seemed to know you quite well, too . . . told me a few of your guilty secrets."

"I didn't think I had any. Right. Two more minutes and it'll be ready. Meantime, I haven't been greeted with a kiss yet."

"No time for frivolity," she began, but he ignored her and once more, drew her into his arms. A few moments later, she pulled away and when she spoke, her voice was husky.

"I could get addicted to this . . ."

"I'm working on it," Adam said softly, but then took a brisker tone when he added, "Now take a seat and dig in."

They chatted easily during the meal and

as he watched her talking animatedly about her wedding dress design, he smiled as he thought of a possible future together — and this time it wasn't just in fashion.

"I've been putting together some more ideas for your website," he told her. "But I'll continue working on it till you've finished the dress. I suspect you're going to be busy for the next few days."

"I really can't think of anything else at the moment. This feels like the first really big chance I've had and I don't want to mess it up. The food was delicious, Adam, but I ought to get on."

"You go back upstairs. I'll wash up."

"You really are too good to be true. A man who cooks *and* washes up. How come you haven't been snapped up long ago?"

"I wouldn't do it for just anyone, you know. And the right person hasn't snapped at me yet!"

As she went back to her work, Sophie frowned. What was he saying? Surely he couldn't possibly be hinting at what she thought? He didn't know her at all and she didn't know him except on a very superficial basis.

She liked him a lot, of that there was no doubt, but he seemed to be moving things along much too quickly for comfort.

Half an hour later, he arrived with a cup of coffee.

"Don't worry, it's de-caff if you were worried that you'd drunk too much coffee today. I've also brought you chocolate — for energy, of course, purely medicinal." He laid the coffee and chocolate on a side table and said, "Is it all right if I sit up here and watch you? Talk a little?"

"I'm afraid I won't be much company; my brain's working overtime, a bit too focussed . . . actually, could you look in the cupboard on the landing, please? There should be a dressmaker's dummy stored in there."

"I knew I'd have my uses," he said and went off to fetch it.

He watched fascinated as she fitted pieces of the flimsy fabric to the dummy and tacked it together. "How do you know it's the right size?" he asked.

"It's just a rough guess and it's only quick, loose tacking so I can adjust it on Chloe to get the fit just right. I use the dummy to hold it in shape while I'm working."

"Have you ever made anything for children?" he asked.

"Only for friends. Why?"

"I was just wondering if you should produce some kids' clothes as well; it would make a nice feature for the show."

"Not the dreaded mother and daughter look-alikes," she laughed. "I can't tell you how much I hate them!"

"No, but you could have some sort of theme; garments made in the same colours as a sort of set piece."

"You're really getting quite carried away, aren't you?"

"Actually, it was Marnie's idea. I was chatting to her today and told her you were doing Chloe's wedding dress. They were at school together so she's looking forward to having Chloe living nearby when they go to America. Alex is going to the New York office, too, so he'll be working with Marnie."

"Not Alex from finance?"

"One and the same."

"It strikes me that you're related to just about everyone connected with the firm."

"Not quite — but I'm working on it." He grinned broadly.

"Anyway, how could you tell Marnie I was doing the wedding dress? You didn't know if Chloe would agree."

"Of course I did. Chloe would never turn you down, especially not if I suggested you."

"You're very presumptuous, aren't you?"

"Just confident." He grinned again. "But I think I'd better leave you to it. I seem to be slowing down your progress."

"You are a bit of a distraction." Realising what she'd implied, she quickly added, "I really appreciate what you're doing for me Adam, and for coming round to feed me, but . . ."

"It's okay, I'm off now. But just one thing — please, will you lock your door after me? You mustn't leave it open the way you do. It may be a remote place, but anyone can just walk in and I'm worried after the broken window."

They went downstairs together and he insisted on sharing a goodnight kiss, although she didn't put up much opposition.

She ignored the warning bells that kept ringing but she was enjoying it too much. He was certainly something very special, this Adam Gilbert, even if he did seem too good to be true.

While she wandered back upstairs to her work, she wondered where else could she find a man who was interested in fashion, able to cook and willing to help her start a business of her own? And exactly why was she so set on a no-strings relationship anyway? Surely at twenty-four, she was quite old enough to have whatever sort of relationship she chose?

"You're just plain scared, Sophie James,"

she told herself aloud. "Scared of commitment, scared of being hurt again." The
dressmaker's dummy made no comment
and Sophie gave a small sigh and went back
to her shaping, pinning and tacking.

It was past midnight before she called it a
day and tumbled into bed feeling exhausted
but satisfied.

She needed to make an early start the next
day if she was to be ready for Chloe's visit
later in the morning. She needed to draw
and paint the final design before they chose
the perfect fabric from the samples they had
picked out yesterday.

All too soon, it was midday and Chloe's arrival was imminent. Sophie put the kettle
on and made some coffee, realising that she
didn't even have a biscuit to offer her visitor. She rarely ate such things herself and
hoped Chloe felt the same.

She heard a car stop and went to the door.

"Hi," Chloe called. "What a lovely spot
you have here — but aren't you scared, being so remote?"

"Not at all. Everyone asks that." Sophie
smiled. "Come on in. I've just made coffee
if you'd like some."

They went upstairs to the workroom and
Chloe looked around in amazement.

"This is so cool," she said. "All these gorgeous period clothes. Adam told me this was what you do. They're fantastic. Can I have a look after we're done?"

"Of course you can. I've made a start as you can see. I need to fit the bodice properly first. At least you won't have time to change your shape between now and the wedding," Sophie said. "You'd be amazed at how many brides buy a size smaller because they plan to lose weight. I had a friend who ran a bridal shop and I used to help her during holidays."

They got to work and soon the pieces were marked to fit perfectly. It was a simple style with a rounded neckline and straight sleeves, and the skirt had a flat panel at the front flaring into a gently pleated rear so it made maximum impact from the back during the service.

"With the heavier fabric you've chosen, this will look stunning," Sophie assured the bride. "And it shows off your slender figure perfectly. Do you plan to wear a veil?"

"Just a small one, I thought. Perhaps with fresh flowers as a head dress?"

"That's perfect, since I wouldn't want it to cover the lacing I plan for the back. Look, I did a sketch." Sophie held it out.

"Oh, that's so lovely! And what's this?"

Chloe pointed.

"A line of small pearls to pick out the shaping. I'll do some more pearls and bead-work on the bodice. Now all I need to do is buy the fabric you've chosen from the samples."

"Let's go together this afternoon. I want to see it all the way through," Chloe enthused. "And I need to give you a deposit to at least pay for the fabric."

"Thanks," Sophie said gratefully. How could she have been so unprofessional as to forget to ask? If it had been anyone other than a personal contact, she could have been out of pocket to the tune of several hundreds of pounds.

They went in Chloe's car and she drove her back to the cottage, complete with large parcels of fabric and all the trimmings for completing the job.

"I'll need to see you again in a couple of days," Sophie told her. "For another fitting."

"I can't wait. Actually . . . just how busy are you?"

"It depends what you were thinking."

"I have four little bridesmaids and one matron of honour to dress. I was going to buy something off the peg for them but it would be terrific if you could make their dresses as well."

Five more dresses? Sophie gulped slightly. It would make a terrific wedding ensemble for the show's finale, though.

"Well, we have three clear weeks before the big day. Presumably the children are small?"

"All under seven," Chloe replied hopefully. "I may regret so many excited little girls but I had to ask them all, you know how it is. The matron of honour is about my size but I'm thinking something simple but in strong colours to make an impact?"

"Okay," Sophie agreed. "I'll sketch something out for you but obviously, until I've seen them, it will only be ideas."

"Great! I'll see you in a couple of days and we can make the plans for the rest. I'm so proud to be a part in the start of your new business, Sophie."

Sophie said goodbye, feeling a bit shell-shocked at what she was taking on. But this was what she wanted to do with her life and she knew she could make just about anything anyone wanted. She glanced at her watch. It was almost five o'clock. She couldn't wait to make a start, and took all the purchases up to her workroom, where she cleared the table and took out the heavy, ivory satin they had chosen.

The fabric was perfect for her design and

she fingered it, longing to start working with it, even though the hugely expensive cost gave her a few nerves when she finally plunged the scissors into it.

The muslin shapes were the pattern and soon, she was piling up the pieces into the large plastic crate she used to keep individual projects together. She had almost finished cutting the bodice when she heard a car stop outside.

Surely Adam couldn't be coming to spend yet another evening with her? For once she had locked the door, so she went down to see who was there.

"Adam," she said as she let him in. "What a surprise."

"I come bearing gifts. I assume you haven't eaten?"

"Well, no . . . I was just thinking about it."

"I've brought pizza and there's salad to go with it."

"That sounds great but you must stop feeding me. Don't you have anything more important to do with your time?"

"Certainly not. Getting to know you is the most important thing in my life at present. And I'm bearing in mind what you said about us. I have to slow things down and take my time and take on board any other conditions you want to impose."

"Well, thank you. I'm glad you see it that way."

"I took advice from the Wise One."

Sophie laughed. "And who is that exactly?"

"My sister, Marnie, of course."

"What on earth did you say to her?" Sophie was beginning to feel a little uncomfortable about being discussed.

"I just said I was really keen to get to know you properly and she immediately said that I shouldn't be rushing into anything."

"Wise words indeed. Our lives are getting a bit involved on so many levels, Adam. I need to take it one step at a time."

"Well, I was making plans for Saturday and I thought that maybe you could come over to my place and have a swim. Then in the evening, we could go to a new club I've heard is rather good. What do you think?"

"It depends how I get on with all this work. Apart from the dress, Chloe wants me to make five bridesmaids' dresses now. I have to be single-minded if it's going to be done in time."

"Well, that's great news. But I insist you take a short break."

"But I'll have to do fittings for the bridesmaids — and Saturday may be the only time they can come."

"Okay, then; Saturday evening, we'll go to the club, if they come during the day, and you can come over on Sunday morning for that swim. In fact, that might be best. Then you can stay for Sunday lunch with my parents; they always make a thing of Sunday lunch with the family."

Sophie was astonished. "And what was that about not rushing things? Yet here you are introducing me to the family in practically the same breath."

"But you've already met my parents and you'll have met Bee and her two daughters by then; they're two of the bridesmaids."

"Do you know who the others are? There are four little ones and one adult."

"Ah, I suspect that might be Rachel . . ."

"Oh, dear — if it is Rachel, she won't be at all happy about having something home-made by me."

"Don't worry about it. She doesn't get to choose. You're letting that lack of confidence show again."

"Sorry." Sophie flushed. "But this is such a big deal for me. I have to make it work."

The thought of any contact with Rachel was not something she would choose. She needed to steel herself for the meeting.

CHAPTER 6

Adam left soon after they'd eaten and Sophie realised with a slight pang that he hadn't kissed her goodbye. Even though it was exactly what she had demanded, she missed it.

She tried to tell herself it was the most sensible way if the business was to be launched.

Was she ready to meet his family? Not really, but the temptation was there, especially as some of them were involved in this wedding. It might be nice to have a break but it depended on how hard she worked in the meantime.

By the following evening, the bodice was almost complete, apart from the pearl trimmings which would be added after the final fitting. The skirt was cut out and the panels partly stitched together, enough to show the finished lines.

Feeling totally exhausted, she stopped sewing for the night and sketched some basic designs for the bridesmaids.

Adam usually seemed to arrive well before six-thirty if he was coming but he seemed to have taken her at her word and was slowing things down. She gave a shrug and delved in the freezer for a ready meal. She had just finished when the phone rang.

"Have you eaten?" asked Adam.

"I have, thank you."

"Just checking. How was your day?"

"Good, thanks. I made progress and I'm just about to do some sketches for the bridesmaids' dresses."

"I just thought I'd warn you that the adult bridesmaid is indeed Rachel. Evidently, she volunteered herself and Chloe didn't have the courage to say no. And I'm to be the best man, by the way. I suspect this is why Rachel pushed herself forward. She has this weird thing about me . . ."

Sophie could almost hear him shudder on the other end of the phone. "But you needn't worry; I'll make sure you're sitting near to me."

"Hang on. I haven't actually been invited to this wedding."

"Well of course you will be," he told her. "If not in your own right as the dress designer, then certainly as my guest."

"Your 'and other' again, I suppose," she said, remembering how this all got started in the first place.

"Would it be okay if I come round tomorrow evening?" he asked. "I thought you might need an evening off from me today but I wanted to be sure you'd eaten some-thing."

"I'm a big girl now, but it was nice of you to phone."

"I'll see you tomorrow, then?"

"I'll look forward to seeing you."

She put the phone down and smiled.

It seemed Adam was perfect in every way; even realising she needed some time to her-self.

She put the television on and sat with her sketch pad on her knee, half watching some soap.

Someone was getting married and her mind was so full of wedding details, she looked up and concentrated on what was happening. In the midst of a great deal of angst and people shouting, she took note of a very elegant bridal gown and some slightly frilly children's dresses.

A hideous Barbie pink took away from what were rather sweet dresses for little children. Her pencil flew over the page as she created a much simpler design, giving a softer look to the skirt.

She went up to her workroom and found some fabric scraps in a variety of colours to give Chloe some ideas.

She was just pinning them to the sketches and feeling rather pleased, when she heard a car stop outside and leapt up. Adam must have decided to come over after all.

She went to the door and looked out just as tail lights were disappearing down the track. It looked like the same car that had been there the previous night.

She went back inside, and she realised that she was disappointed that it hadn't been Adam — and was more than slightly perturbed by the strange visitor.

It reminded her that she must get that window fixed.

She picked up her sketch pad again and looked at what she had so far. Rachel's dress would have to be something quite different from the smaller children's dresses. Still, at least she had some ideas to show Chloe.

"Wow, that's terrific!" Chloe encouraged when she saw what had been achieved the following day.

"Sorry, I must get a large mirror in here," Sophie said. "There's one in my room if you'd like to go through."

"This is a dream. You're so clever," Chloe continued to enthuse. "I love the way the fabric falls at the back, so graceful and elegant. I'm going to feel like a princess."

Over cups of tea, they got to the thorny problem of Rachel's dress. It seemed she was going to be as difficult to satisfy as Sophie feared.

"When I said you were making the dresses she positively turned her nose up," Chloe said. "I won't repeat her actual comments but I fear she isn't going to be easy to please."

"I can imagine. She was pretty unpleasant to me at the other wedding. I gather she was hoping for something to develop between her and Adam and I got in the way?"

"I guess so. But if she doesn't like it, she can back down," Chloe said with a pout. "I never wanted her in the first place but she made it impossible to say no."

"What colours were you thinking of for the bridesmaids?"

"I wanted a bright colour, nothing pastel or wishy-washy."

They spent some time discussing options and finally decided to arrange another visit to the fabric shop.

"Rachel's colouring limits us a bit," Sophie advised. "Reds and pinks and lilacs might be a bit dodgy."

"Can we meet at the shop tomorrow morning? I've got to get it sorted before the afternoon as I have an appointment with the florist. My list of things to do is about three miles long."

They met again the following morning at the fabric shop. After much debating, they finally decided on a bright, sky-blue, silky fabric that would suit the four little girls as well as Rachel. They decided to buy it there and then, with Sophie estimating quantities even before the final design was chosen.

"I want to check out your recycled clothes next time, too, if that's all right?" Chloe asked. "I'd love some of them to take to New York. They'll go down a storm there."

"I can see I'll have to start over for my fashion show."

"I'll be a walking advertisement for you in New York," Chloe said. "You need a designer logo all of your own. Get Adam to do one for you — he's very good at that kind of thing."

Chloe then went off to the florist with a sample of the fabric and a whole new set of ideas.

Sophie shook her head slightly. It seemed however quickly it had been arranged, this wedding was going to have the full works. If she'd been in a similar position, she felt certain she would have gone for something very simple with minimum fuss. But then, this was a large family, none of whom would ever skimp on anything.

That evening, Adam arrived at six-thirty promptly and complete with an Indian take-away. "I hope you like curry," he said. "I never asked but took a gamble."

"So long as it isn't too hot. Look, tomorrow, you must let me either take you out or cook something. I can't keep relying on you for meals."

"Nonsense. I want to keep you sewing, you see. Things are moving in the big wide world and we have to be ready for this show of ours."

"Ours?" Sophie raised one eyebrow suspiciously.

"Sorry." Adam was suddenly a little sheepish. "Just trying to be encouraging."

"Oh, before I forget . . . according to Chloe, I need a logo. She said you're good at that sort of thing."

"Okay," he said, regaining his enthusiam. "We need a name."

"What about something like 'Style by Sophie'?"

"It needs a bit more impact."

"Just Sophie then," she suggested. "If it's not too corny."

"Let's go with that. I'll play around with

it and see what comes of it. We can work together, if you like."

They sat companionably in the workroom while Sophie sketched and Adam designed her logo on his laptop. He admired the wedding dress as far as it was done.

"I need to fiddle around with some of the bridesmaids' fabric," Sophie explained. "See how it will drape. I'll have to come up with something stunning to satisfy Rachel — oh, and I'll need a large dress bag to carry the wedding dress around."

"I'll look and see what I can find," Adam suggested. He tapped into his laptop and came up with several different suggestions. "There are two here. Not expensive at all and breathable, whatever that's supposed to mean."

"Let me look." She leaned across him and smiled. "Perfect. How do I order them? I ought to buy several for future use."

"Easy. I have an online account. I'll order six, shall I?" He tapped away and a few minutes later, announced the bags were on the way.

"That's incredible. I thought I'd have to trudge round for hours to find anything like that. I must get a decent laptop so I can see what's around."

"I've only just updated mine. My old one

would probably do all you need. I'll bring it round."

"I'll pay for it," she began. "And I owe you for the dress bags you just ordered. We'll have to keep an account."

"Don't be silly," Adam insisted. "I'd only throw out the old laptop. Have you decided about Sunday lunch yet?"

"I'm not sure. I feel a bit apprehensive . . . Let me see how I get on. If it's a nice day, it would be rather nice — but I do have my work cut out to get all this sewing done."

"Fair enough. It's my fault for landing you with it all so I can't complain," Adam conceded.

"I'm more than grateful for everything you're doing. I'm amazed that you're even taking such an interest."

"I want to see you as a successful business-woman in your own right; I think you need the fulfilment. I've seen so many capable people who just sit back and moan they're bored, but not you — if you're bored, you find something to interest you."

"So the people who work in your office are lacking ambition?"

"Some of them, yes."

"But they have to work to pay the bills. We can't all be super heroes, you know. You need workers to keep everything going. And many people do perfectly good jobs and maybe they enjoy something else away from the office," she told him with more passion than she realised she felt about the matter.

"I can't say I was thrilled with my spate of temping," she said, "but I'm glad I could earn some money."

"Touché. You're right, of course. And I'll admit it allows space for genius to show itself."

"Probably. Right, I think that will do for tonight."

"May I see?"

"These are the little girls' dresses. For Rachel, I thought a similar-shaped top to Chloe's dress but without the long train at the back. She's quite skinny really, so I don't want to show the bony parts of her neck in an unflattering way."

"She should like that. You're right, there's slim and there's downright skinny. Clever girl," he encouraged.

He paused and then sighed. "Well, I suppose I should be moving; you've probably got another early start and I have to work. Thank goodness it's Friday tomorrow."

He switched off his computer and packed it away in its case.

They both moved towards the door, almost bumping into each other. There was a moment of embarrassed silence before Adam spoke.

"Sophie . . . oh, Sophie," he murmured as he drew her close.

She found herself completely unable to object and kissed him back.

"Please Adam," she managed to say at last, pushing him away, almost breathless.

"I can't tell you how hard it's been this past couple of days, trying not to touch you. One day, we'll be together properly, you know that. But I do understand that for now, you're not ready."

"Adam . . . I . . ."

"It's all right, I'm going," he told her gently. "I'll call you tomorrow, see how things are going."

"Thank you again for supper," she said softly. "And thank you for being so understanding."

She lay for a long time before sleeping, thinking of Adam and how understanding he was trying to be, of the promise he had made — and of the metres of blue fabric that still awaited her attention. The next few weeks were going to be impossibly busy and the next hurdle was the coming visit of Rachel for her fitting.

When Saturday arrived, it was a glorious,

sunny day. Normally, Sophie would have enjoyed a walk in the woods followed by less enjoyable washing and cleaning and a trip to the supermarket. Thanks to Adam's regular food deliveries, grocery shopping could wait, and the laundry and cleaning would just have to be postponed.

She was expecting the arrival of all the children and their mothers, as well as Rachel and Chloe. Her little cottage would be full to bursting point, but it was important to see them all at the same time, just for this initial meeting. She could get an idea of how they would be together as a group.

She had made several copies of her drawings so they could all see them and finally agree on their favourite styles.

"What a lovely place," Bee declared as her two daughters clambered out of the car. "Adam's told me so much about you. I'm so looking forward to seeing your ideas."

"I hope you won't be disappointed," Sophie said. "Come in. The others will be here soon."

Bee was heavily pregnant and almost immediately confessed that she was hoping that the baby would either come very soon or hang on until after the wedding.

"When are you due?" Sophie asked.

"In about ten days. Hopefully, that gives

me time to get over it and to be able to cope with these two overexcited little girls."

Sophie felt drawn to Bee. She was charming and seemed very down-to-earth. She was similar in colouring to Adam, with bright blue eyes that were perhaps a shade darker than his. The two girls were surprisingly blonde but had the family's blue eyes. The fabric they had bought for the dresses would suit them perfectly. They were clinging shyly to their mother.

"They take after their father," Bee said, noticing Sophie's eyes assessing the group. "Oh, it's so lovely to meet you. I've been intrigued by Adam's sudden interest in fashion but now I begin to see why."

"Thank you . . . I think," Sophie replied, just as another car pulled up outside.

It was Rachel and Chloe. The bride-to-be greeted Sophie warmly and kissed her cheeks, but Rachel stood back with an expression suggesting she would rather be anywhere but here.

"I think you've met Rachel," Chloe said politely. "You must have done, as you knew the way here, Rachel."

"Hello again." Sophie smiled politely to Rachel. "But how did you know where I live?"

Rachel gave a nasty grin before turning

back to Chloe. "We met at Joan's wedding. Amazing to see how she's taking over everything, although I think we all know why." There was a sarcastic edge to Rachel's voice but Chloe spoke again.

"Sophie is amazing, and she's taken a load of worry off me. My dress is a dream — not that any of you are going to see it until the day. You have covered it up, don't you Sophie?"

"Oh, yes. We can't let it get dusty. But I do have some sketches for you all to look at. Chloe has the final word, of course, but I'd like to hear what you all think."

At the sound of yet another car, Chloe offered, "I think Sally and her brood are just arriving. Shall I let them in?"

The little room was crowded with so many people.

They stood round the table where Sophie had put the drawings and samples of the fabric. Chloe produced pictures of the flowers she had chosen; the girls were to have baskets filled with blue and white flowers and there was a hand spray for Rachel which would allow her other hand free to take charge of the bridal bouquet during the service.

By midday, everyone except Rachel was thrilled with the plans. Two at a time,

Sophie took the girls upstairs to the workroom and took copious measurements.

Once they had left, it was Rachel's turn. Fortunately Chloe came upstairs too, and managed to maintain a sort of peace between them.

"So this is it? Your trading stock?" Rachel said with a sneer. "The basis for your so-called fashion show?"

"Some of it may be; it depends how much time I have to complete my range. Chloe has kindly agreed to let me use her dress and I hope the bridesmaids will also take part."

"I'll probably be out of the country," Rachel sniffed. "I'm planning a cruise. Adam had promised to join me until you put a spanner in the works, demanding all his spare time. You're very lucky he's agreed to get you out of this hole."

Sophie bit her tongue from the sharp retort in her mind, but instead said, "If we get some measurements?"

"And I don't like this drawing you've done, not at all. It doesn't show off my best features."

"I see . . . what were you hoping for?"

"You've made it with a high neck for a start and the back is so low it makes a boring line for the congregation to look at during the service."

"But I assumed you'd be seated for much of the service?"

"As Matron of Honour, I shall be very visible. No, I'm afraid it simply won't do. You'll have to think again. I need something sophisticated, stunning, something to get me noticed."

"Actually, Rachel, Chloe is the star of this whole event. You wouldn't want to take away attention from her, would you?" She saw Chloe grinning behind her.

"And this design is perfect for you, Rachel," Chloe agreed. "It will hide your rather bony neck but show off your slim figure. And the little bit of lacing at the rear sort of echoes my dress."

"Really?" Rachel's voice was all exaggerated surprise. "Well, if it's what you want . . . Who am I to complain about your taste? And that sort of draped bit below the bust? Wouldn't that —"

"It's perfect," Chloe interrupted, smiling at Sophie. "You've done a terrific job."

"A matter of opinion," Rachel muttered, just loud enough for Sophie to hear. Why was the woman being so spiteful?

"I think we'd better leave you to it now," Chloe suggested. "I'll come over on Monday as we arranged for the next fitting."

"You'll probably need me again if this isn't going to be a complete disaster," Rachel said. "Only I'm very busy at present and need plenty of notice."

"Next weekend, perhaps?" Sophie offered.

"I'm busy. It will have to be either Thursday evening or the following Monday. There's a house party Adam and I are going to, up in Devon. We have to talk about our roles in this coming wedding."

Chloe frowned at this suggestion. What on earth was there for them to discuss?

"Make it the Monday, then," Sophie said calmly. "I'll work on the girls' dresses first, and I can see them at the weekend."

Once she had the place to herself again, she slumped down, feeling totally exhausted. Her tummy rumbled and she realised she needed food to boost her energy. She heated beans and made toast — comfort food.

She reflected on the morning. The children and their mothers had all been delightful and so excited about their dresses, but Rachel had been even worse than expected. She was going to have to make her dress very special and perfect in every detail if she was to survive without too much criticism.

She wondered again how Rachel knew

where she lived. She thought of the car that had driven away one night. Could she have followed Adam? The woman was certainly obsessed. She also felt niggled that Adam was going away with that awful woman for all of the next weekend.

But she was the one who was afraid of getting too involved too quickly, so what else could she expect? She was being a bit of an ice maiden, wasn't she?

Wearily, she dumped the dishes in the sink and began to make her patterns for the little bridesmaids' dresses. It was going to be a hectic few days.

She looked up as her peace was shattered by the noise of motorbikes. A gang of riders roared through the usually calm woodland, tearing up grass and wild flowers as they went.

She rushed out ready to yell at them, but they had gone.

Not a good sign if this became a habit. Could it be one of them who had broken her window? She still hadn't got it fixed.

CHAPTER 7

Upstairs in her workroom, Sophie was engrossed in her tasks and had already forgotten the noisy bikers.

"How's it going?" said a voice behind her. She nearly jumped out of her skin. "Sorry to startle you, but yet again; you left your door open. One of these days . . ."

"Adam, hi. I didn't think you were coming over today."

"I was anxious to know how you'd got on with everyone."

"Bee is lovely and so are her two girls."

"I take it Rachel wasn't?"

"No. Predictably, she found fault with everything, but Chloe chipped in saying it had been her choice, so she had to shut up and I only have to make a couple of minor changes."

"Good. I came to see how you're getting on, too. Will you manage the club this evening or would you prefer to leave it until next weekend?"

"I thought you were away next weekend? A house party in Devon?" Sophie said with exaggerated casualness.

"Whatever gave you that idea?"

"Rachel announced that you were going together . . . to discuss your roles in this wedding."

"It's the first I've heard of it." At that moment, his mobile phone rang. "Excuse me," he said. "Hello?"

Sophie continued her work, only partly

hearing one side of the conversation. From that, she assumed it was Rachel actually inviting him to accompany her on this weekend jaunt. From his replies, she gathered that he would not even think of going anywhere with her. Interesting that the woman had sold it to Sophie as a fait accompli, trying her best to make her feel jealous, no doubt.

"Honestly. I'll end up saying something unforgivable to that woman one of these days. I don't know why she persists when I've made it quite clear I have no feelings for her at all — except anger and annoyance."

"Oh, dear. Poor woman. She totally blames me for spoiling things between you, you know."

"There never was anything between me and Rachel to spoil. I'm just sorry you have to be involved with her at all."

"By the way, do you think she could have followed you last week? Only Chloe said she knew where I live, but this was her first visit."

"It's possible, I suppose. We did see a car that looked familiar. It's a bit weird, though."

"I think Chloe is getting a bit fed up with her."

"Not surprising. Look, I suspect you'd prefer to work on for a while, wouldn't you?" Sophie nodded. "Shall I leave you to it, or can I hang around?"

"You could always ply me with cups of tea. It's nice to have you around — but won't you get terribly bored?"

"I've got my laptop so I can get on with things."

It was a pleasant, companionable afternoon. They played some music and at one point, decided they needed some fresh air and took a walk in the woods.

"Being with you like this feels so right," Adam said suddenly. "Don't you feel it, too?"

"Well yes, I do, actually. You're always so thoughtful and seem to know when I need space to myself."

"So why do I feel as if you're fighting me off all the time?"

"I . . . well . . . I made a big mistake once . . . I allowed someone to get too close and thought I loved him and believed it was the whole package. We even got engaged . . ." She looked down at her ring finger as if it was bringing back painful memories.

"And what happened?" Adam prompted gently.

"We planned to get married but a month

before the wedding, he went off with one of my best friends. She was to have been my chief bridesmaid as it happens, so I'm finding the Rachel situation almost too much in a way. I know now he wasn't right for me and he tried to take over everything I was doing. I suppose this whole situation is reminding me of something I'd tried to put behind me."

"So getting you involved with this wedding might not have been my brightest idea?" Adam looked worried.

"No, no — I'm delighted to have this chance. Oh, don't mind me. I'm probably just overtired."

"It helps explain things — but don't tar me with the same brush. With me and Jess, it never reached that point. The getting married thing was never on the cards, and I always knew she wasn't the once-and-forever person."

"How do you know — I mean, really know — when you've found that once-and-forever person?"

"It's a gut feeling, I guess. You think of them all the time and until you're secure that your feelings are reciprocated, you want to keep checking up on them, being with them, spending every possible waking hour in their company."

"You make it sound as if you've been there."

"Perhaps . . . perhaps I am . . ."

"Adam, if you're saying what I think you're saying . . . I'm becoming very fond of you but . . . well, we've only known each other such a short time. Don't try to . . ."

"I know. Don't worry, I'm not trying to rush you. And I'll try not to be a control freak. Sometimes though, we need to do things together — ordinary things like this, being companionable. I promise, though, I won't say any more until you're ready."

"I'm beginning to think you really are too good to be true."

"Of course I'm not . . . well, maybe I am!" He laughed. "How about we go down to your little pub and have a bar snack and then I'll leave you to hack your fabrics into little pieces — on condition you come and join us at my place tomorrow. Bee is coming with the kids and her husband. You did say you liked her. What do you think?"

"Okay — I suppose I do need a break."

"Great! Come over around eleven tomorrow. That should give us time to enjoy the pool first. The kids will probably want to swim as well, so be prepared. You can get back to your sewing machine after lunch if you want to."

They enjoyed a quick meal at the pub before Adam drove home, leaving her with a couple of hours before bedtime to finish her work.

She noticed her answering machine was flashing and pressed the button for the message but all she heard was deep breathing before the call was dropped. She gave a shiver and went to lock the door.

She took the time to make herself a proper plan for the next few days and could see that she would easily complete everything before the next fittings. Exhausted, she'd no sooner fallen into a deep sleep than the phone rang. She dragged herself out of her slumber and picked it up.

"Hello?" she murmured. There was more of the deep breathing and suddenly a voice hissed.

"Give it up."

It was a husky, deep sound and later, she wasn't sure if she had heard actual words among the hissing sounds.

She lay awake for so long that she was beginning to wonder if it had been a dream.

Next morning Sophie packed up her swimming things and drove towards Rayman's Creek.

The cul-de-sac had very large houses and

expensive looking bungalows, clearly top executive territory.

She felt conscious that her modest little car was somewhat out of place among such wealth but she took a deep breath and drove into the parking space.

Nervously, she rang the doorbell, hoping she'd got the right place. Adam had told her that his flat was attached to the main house but it wasn't obvious which was his door.

His mother answered the bell. "Hello Sophie. I'm pleased you could join us. Do come in. I think Adam is still in his flat."

"Thank you, Mrs Gilbert. What a lovely house you have." *Damn,* Sophie thought; she should have brought flowers.

They walked through a huge and charmingly furnished sitting room onto a terrace that overlooked the garden.

Long lawns went down towards the creek itself and a small landing stage had a boat moored to it. The swimming pool was to one side and seemed to go on forever.

"What a wonderful garden and the trees are just perfect."

"Thank you, my dear. We do love it here, private and secluded. Most of the land bordering the creek is privately owned so we don't get too much traffic along the waterway. Can I get you something . . . wine, coffee?"

"Coffee would be lovely, thank you."

"I'll give Adam a call to let him know you're here and I'll bring coffee out. Bee and the children are on their way over so make the most of a few minutes' peace."

Sophie sat back in the comfortable chair and continued to look around. The whole place was out of this world — out of her world, at least.

She turned to smile as Adam came in.

"Sophie, I'm so sorry. I didn't realise you'd arrived. I hope Mum's been looking after you?"

"Yes, she's making coffee. What a wonderful home."

"We love it. I'll show you my flat in a minute. But you look tired — is everything all right?"

"I'm fine, really, I just didn't sleep too well." She decided not to tell him about the phone call.

Mrs Gilbert arrived at that point with the coffee. "Oh good, my son's stirred himself at last. I brought coffee for you too, Adam. Bee and the others are just arriving."

"Great. We'll drink this and get ready for the pool. I expect the brats will want to try drowning me as usual."

"I'm not a very good swimmer," Sophie said anxiously.

"Don't worry, neither are they. We have plenty of floats; blow up bananas are easy to race on!"

"By the way, Adam," Mrs Gilbert interrupted. "You might have told me you'd invited Rachel over today. She just called to ask what time lunch is served."

"I didn't invite her, Mum. Actually, she's driving me mad just now with her constant calling. In fact, I'm going to phone and un-invite her!"

He went inside and Sophie heard his angry words as he spoke on the telephone. "No, you were not invited, Rachel. This is a family day with my sister . . ." He paused. "Frankly, it's none of your business whether Sophie is here or not . . . stop pestering me, Rachel . . . Goodbye."

Soon they were all splashing around in the pool and Sophie was able to put the whole business with Rachel out of her mind.

Bee was sitting in the shade looking rather pale, while her husband, Dennis, was in the water with the children, having a good time. After a while, Sophie decided to sit with Bee and keep her company.

"They're all a bit rough, aren't they?" Bee smiled. "Mum's in the kitchen and Dad's probably speaking to Marnie on Skype and having a catch-up . . ." She gave a slight sigh.

"Are you all right?" Sophie asked anxiously.

"I'm not feeling too good, actually. I've been having a few twinges but I assumed they were Braxton Hicks contractions."

"What are they?"

"Little pains towards the end of pregnancy, like a false labour . . . but maybe this isn't a false start . . ." She winced.

"I thought you had a couple more weeks to go?"

"Well, it's always a bit uncertain . . . don't worry, though, I took hours with the girls. Even if I am starting, it'll be ages before I actually give birth."

"All the same, shouldn't I call someone? Your husband?"

"No, leave him with the girls; he's no good at these sort of things . . ." She winced again. "But maybe I will tell Mum."

"I'll go," Sophie jumped up. "Which way is the kitchen?"

Bee made no reply, but groaned slightly instead, so Sophie dashed inside and called for Adam's mother. She could smell roast meat cooking and followed her nose.

"Mrs Gilbert? Mrs Gilbert! I think you

should come! I think Bee has started labour."

"Oh, heavens!" she called. "She isn't due for another two weeks. She's been doing too much. I'd better call the doctor."

When Sophie returned to the terrace, Bee was lying back in her chair while the noise from the pool continued unabated. Sophie stood quietly watching her for a few moments until Bee opened her eyes.

"I think this is the real thing. You'd better call Dennis. Perhaps Adam can . . ." She broke off as a new contraction took over and she flashed Sophie a tight smile.

Sophie didn't have a clue what she should be doing but she ran down to the pool edge and waved at Dennis.

"It's Bee," she cried out. "I think the baby's coming!"

Dennis leapt out of the pool and told Sophie, "Keep the girls occupied, will you? Adam will help; he's great with them."

Sophie shed the robe and jumped back into the water.

Adam quickly swam over to her. "What's up?"

"It's the baby. Bee's started but Dennis wants us to look after the girls. Bee says it will take ages anyway."

"What's happening?" asked the younger

child, Heidi.

"Mummy's not feeling too good so Daddy's gone to look after her," Adam told her calmly.

"I want to go too. Mummy will need me," she wailed.

"Better if we stay here. Shall we have another banana race?"

The little girl looked back anxiously; she was clearly distressed and didn't want to stay with her uncle.

"Is the baby coming?" Phoebe, the older child asked.

"We're not sure yet," Sophie answered honestly.

"Will we still be bridesmaids even if Mummy has a new baby?" wailed Heidi, her eyes filling with tears.

"Of course you will," Sophie reassured her. "Now come and show me how these banana float things work."

For the next half hour, Adam and Sophie tried to keep the children's attention away from the activity near the house. All was well until an ambulance arrived and Heidi wailed anxiously, "Where are they taking Mummy?"

"It's all right," Sophie called. "Be a brave girl for your mummy and let's go and see if your gran has lunch ready yet."

Once the girls were dry and dressed again, Adam sent them on ahead into the kitchen.

"I'm sorry you've had all this on your first visit. I'd no idea things were so close. Let's go and see how Mum's coping." He looked rather worried.

"Perhaps she'd prefer it if I went home. A stranger in the midst of a crisis isn't easy."

"Nonsense. You're hardly a stranger. It's just that the ambulance arrived rather quickly and I'm wondering why Dennis didn't just drive her to the hospital himself."

Once they got to the kitchen, which seemed to be the centre of everything, Adam asked his mother about his sister.

"There was no time for the doctor or midwife to get here. It was all happening so quickly I decided to call an ambulance right away . . . do keep it from the children, though."

"Is there anything we can do? Sophie was worried you might think she was in the way but I said she was fine, isn't she?"

"But of course — and there's heaps of food now, too."

During a somewhat stressful meal, with everyone worried about Bee, they tried to keep the girls calm.

"Why don't we know what's happening?" Phoebe asked.

"We'll hear as soon as there's any news," Mrs Gilbert told them. "Daddy will call when something happens."

"I wanted to watch the new baby being born," Phoebe told them. "Mummy said I might be able to. He's going to come out of Mummy's tummy, you know."

"How can he?" demanded Heidi. "Is there a zip or something? I've never seen it if there is."

"If only," Mrs Gilbert sighed and the tension was broken as everyone laughed.

"How would it be if we took a little trip in the boat when we've finished lunch?" Adam suggested. "We can go along the creek and see if there are any ducklings."

"I'd rather wait for some news about Mummy," Phoebe said.

"Well, I could take my mobile and as soon as Daddy phones here, Grandma can call us to let us know. How about that? It will probably take a long time before your new little brother arrives."

Mrs Gilbert encouraged them to make the trip in the boat, if only to get them away from the house for a while. She was clearly feeling anxious about her daughter and didn't want the girls to overhear any possible bad news.

It was a small power boat but it felt stable

and comfortable and Adam drove it at a steady pace so they were able to watch several families of ducklings paddling under the trees that lined the banks.

"We should have brought some crusts for them," Sophie said. "They're very sweet, aren't they? This is so lovely. Another face of Cornwall, entirely."

"You really love it here, don't you?" Adam was watching her face and enjoying her pleasure vicariously.

"Of course I do. There are so many contrasts; the wild north coast with high cliffs and crashing waves, the more gentle south coast with sandy beaches, the moors and sheltered valleys, private creeks like this one. It's a county of such diversity."

"Are you working for the tourist board in your spare time?" Adam laughed good-naturedly.

"Why hasn't your phone rung yet?" Phoebe asked.

"Because nobody's called it because there's no news yet."

"Mummy's taking an awfully long time to fetch our new brother," Heidi pouted.

"We said it might be a long time and it hasn't been all that long yet, really." Sophie did her best to comfort the little girls but they were clearly very worried.

"Let's go back now, then," Adam suggested. "We'll see if Grandma has any ice cream, shall we?"

"We're not allowed to eat between meals," Heidi said primly.

"I think today is probably a special day and your Mummy won't mind one bit if you have an extra ice cream."

It felt like a very long afternoon while they were waiting for news. Sophie had planned to leave soon after lunch but felt her presence may be needed to help keep the children occupied.

"I was going to show Sophie my flat," Adam told the girls. "Would you like to come too?"

"Yes please, Uncle Adam! Can we play with your computer?"

"We'll see . . . come on then."

But there was still no news from the hospital and the tension was growing.

CHAPTER 8

Sophie immediately loved Adam's flat. Set to one side of the main house, it was on two floors and hardly qualified for the term "flat". A large sitting room overlooked the garden and pool, with wide doors opening onto the communal terrace. The comfortable kitchen-diner had ample space for entertaining and looked very well equipped.

"It's lovely," she said. "And you've got the best views, too."

"Please can we play computer games?" the girls asked.

"All right but be careful and don't press just any old buttons." He led them into his small study, switched on one of several computers and set up a simple game for them. "Okay? You know how to play this one, don't you?"

They were soon engrossed and Adam beckoned Sophie back to the kitchen. "Tea or coffee?" he asked.

"Tea would be great, thanks. It's odd we haven't heard anything, isn't it?"

"These things take time. I think both the girls took ages."

"Yes, Bee told me that, but she looked as if she was well on the way and what with the ambulance and everything —"

Just then Adam's mobile phone rang.

"Yes, Mum, I see . . . Yes . . . we'll keep them here for a bit . . . okay, Mum."

He snapped his mobile shut and turned to Sophie. "All's well. Bee's still waiting but the problems they feared have subsided."

He sighed and told Sophie, "Apparently they thought they might have to do an emergency C-section but she's progressing normally again."

He passed a mug of tea across the counter top. "Mum wants us to keep the girls here for a bit while she collects Bee's things from her home. Dennis is staying at the hospital with her till the baby arrives."

"We'd better tell them, though, hadn't we?"

"Well, they don't know how long it might take," Adam explained, "And it's probably just as well not to worry the girls until we know more ourselves."

As it was, it wasn't too long before they had the good news that all had gone well and the baby was born.

Eventually, the girls were put to bed, amidst great excitement once they knew their baby brother had arrived safely. They had been promised that they could see him early the following day if they went to bed at Grandma's house and behaved themselves.

Sophie eventually arrived back at her home well after nine o'clock, not exactly as intended. Her carefully planned schedule was running well behind.

But she was far too tired to do any work and went to bed early, assuming she would wake early — but it was almost ten o'clock when she came to next day, wakened by her phone.

"Are you all right?" Adam asked. "You took ages to answer."

"I can't believe I slept so long!" Sophie gasped. "Now I'm really behind, seriously off my target."

"I just wanted to thank you for helping out yesterday. Bee and the baby are fine. They're calling him George, and Mum's taken the girls to see them, then they're going to school — rather late but under the circumstances, I'm sure they'll be forgiven." He paused and his tone changed. "Are you sure you're all right?"

"Yes, of course," she told him. "I'll have to work extra hard this week to reach the point I was supposed to be at, though. So don't you go tempting me to go out somewhere!"

"No problem," he laughed. "I'll just bring you food and I promise I'll sit quietly! If that's okay?"

"I'd like that, but I'm sure you must have better things to do."

"I do have to go away to a conference in the middle of the week but I can come tonight and tomorrow." His tone softened as he added, "I'll miss you . . ."

Sophie felt a glow of pure pleasure as she told him, "I'll look forward to seeing you tonight, then."

She took time to think about how her luck had turned. Here she was, doing what she most wanted to do — and she had Adam encouraging her. However hard she needed to work, she was following her dream. It was something she had always talked about but never knew how to start before she met Adam.

She had almost completed the wedding dress, with just a few finishing touches to be added after the final fitting. Rachel's dress was well underway and the children's dresses were ready for a final fitting at the weekend.

Adam had kept his promise of coming over with food for the first two nights and had even left things in the fridge for her for while when he was away.

"You really are spoiling me," she had said before he left. "You really don't need to look after me so much, you know."

"I'm protecting my investment!" he said with a wry grin. "Seriously, Sophie I care about you. I really do want to be a part of your future."

■ ■ ■ ■

Twice more during the week Sophie received strange phone calls, and she eventually decided to unplug her phone each night so she wasn't disturbed.

She admitted to herself that she was missing Adam and wished he was there to talk to. She tried hard to put the whole thing out of her mind and concentrate on the task at hand and getting all these dresses finished on time.

Happily, Chloe was thrilled with her dress when she visited for her final fitting. She stood in Sophie's bedroom, looking in the long mirror and beaming radiantly. "You really are so clever! It's perfect, Sophie, just perfect."

"Let's try the veil you've bought. Are you having your hair up or down?" Sophie asked, swinging into professional mode.

"Decisions, decisions," Chloe laughed.

"I didn't want you to hide that back view and this veil you chose works well," Sophie agreed as she made adjustments.

"So how's Rachel's dress working out?"

"Good, I think, but no doubt she'll find fault with it."

"I'll try to come with her and hopefully

spare you some of her venom. I'm really sorry I asked her to be Matron of Honour," Chloe sighed. "Or at least, I'm sorry that I agreed when she demanded it and now it's as if she's still trying to take over. She'll upset the little ones if she keeps trying to reorganise everything I've already done."

"I'll be around to help get them ready on the big day, if you like," Sophie offered.

"Oh, yes, of course — but you'll be at the wedding anyway, won't you?" Chloe bit her bottom lip anxiously. "Oh, heavens! I never did get around to sending you a proper invitation, did I?"

"No, but I wasn't expecting to be more than the dresser."

"Nonsense," Chloe said. "You'll be with Adam, of course."

"That's very kind of you, thank you. But it won't please Rachel, will it?" she said with a grimace.

"Maybe I can trip her up or something before the day — and then you can take her place . . ." Chloe's face lit up with a mischievous grin. "Actually, that's not a bad idea! How about you being a second matron of honour? Could you make another dress in time?"

"Oh, Chloe, you don't want me. We hardly know each other."

"I already know you better than Rachel — and I like you a whole lot more! If you can make another matching dress in time, I really would be delighted, Sophie."

After Chloe had left, Sophie shook her head in disbelief . . . a second matron of honour? She tried to tell herself it was a ridiculous idea as she finished the stitching on the wedding dress and hung it carefully in one of the large bags that had arrived the previous day.

"One down, five to go . . . or maybe six," she murmured.

Maybe it wasn't such a bad idea, after all, but could she make it on time? If she took up Chloe's suggestion, she would need to buy more fabric, which meant going into Truro right away or it might have been sold.

And if she did buy more, it would be quite a commitment. She could make a dress for herself more easily, though.

She made her decision and, as she got into her car and drove to town, she knew Rachel was going to be furious — and the very thought made her smile.

Saturday was another busy day. All four little girls were visiting for their fittings. Bee wasn't there, of course, but Adam took the opportunity to bring his two little nieces.

"I missed you," he said as soon as he stepped into the cottage, giving her a swift peck on the cheek and telling her, "I'll see you properly later. I've got heaps of news to tell you."

Once the girls were pinned into their dresses and ordered not to wriggle or they'd get pricked by the pins, Sophie took them down to stand in a row outside the cottage.

They looked perfect, with the little coronets of flowers Chloe had ordered and baskets of flowers to complete the picture. Adam took pictures of them all and made them practise standing still for the wedding itself.

"How many more sleeps till Chloe's wedding?" Heidi asked.

"Nine more sleeps," Adam told her, laughing.

"Sleeps?" Sophie asked, bemused.

"It's how they talk about Christmas coming," Adam explained. "It's evidently easier to understand than actual days. I suppose it makes sense really; how do you count the day that's part way through when you're only four?"

"Isn't it a bit unusual to have the wedding on a Tuesday?" Sophie asked.

"It was something to do with the venue being available."

"Did Chloe tell you about her latest idea?" Sophie ventured with more than a little trepidation.

"What's that?"

"That I should share matron of honour duties . . ."

"Oh, what an excellent idea! Rachel will be totally cheesed off, of course, but it does mean I can legitimately be your partner." He paused and grinned broadly, "Are you making another dress the same as Rachel's, then?"

"Hopefully, but don't say too much yet in case I don't have time. I've bought extra fabric, so if I think I can make it, I will." Sophie smiled back at Adam then turned to the girls. "Right, girls, let's get you back inside the cottage and unpinned. I'll see you all again next weekend just before the wedding, to make sure everything's ready."

Once the dresses were safely off, Adam crammed his nieces into the back of his car and drove away.

No sooner had they all gone than Chloe phoned. "How did it go, Sophie?"

"They all looked gorgeous," she told her. "Adam took some pictures so you can see the effect. I was wondering, actually . . . if you have a spare moment would you be able to buy four little dolls . . . Barbies or

131

something?"

"I think I could manage that. Why?"

"I thought I'd make them each a doll dressed in the same outfits as their own."

"That's such a lovely idea!" Chloe enthused. "I'd been wondering what to get for them as bridesmaids' gifts. I had thought of necklaces, but a doll would be something they can really enjoy. But will you have time?"

"I've actually managed to catch up, so I'm up to date."

"And the dress for you . . . ?" Chloe ventured.

"Yes, I'll do that too," Sophie replied.

"I can't believe you! It would take me weeks just to do one dress and here you are making whole rows of frocks in just a fortnight! Anyway, better go — I'll see you Monday evening with Rachel. I haven't told her yet that you'll be taking a role in this wedding. We'll tell her together, shall we?"

"We'd better get the fitting over first then," Sophie suggested, hoping she wasn't storing up trouble for herself.

Sophie spent the rest of the morning sewing on the tiny buttons that were the final touches for the little girls' dresses. Another session and they would be complete.

She glanced at her watch and realised she had missed lunch. She'd been secretly hoping Adam would come back but, apart from hinting that he had lots to tell her, that was it.

She hadn't been grocery shopping for ages, so maybe that had better be the next priority; not a pleasant thought for a Saturday afternoon, but needs must. The shops were crowded and the shelves emptying fast. She flung necessities into her trolley and swiftly decided she'd had enough.

When she arrived back home, Adam's car was parked outside. She pulled the shopping out of the boot and went to unlock the door, but it was already open.

"Adam?" she called.

"I came in and made myself at home," he said in a tone that implied criticism.

"Oh, dear. Did I leave it unlocked again?"

"You really need taking in hand!" He smiled but his tone was worried. "Anyone could have come in. And you still haven't got that window repaired."

"Nobody could climb in through that tiny window," she replied uncertainly. "But you're right, I should have locked the door, especially with all the work I'm doing."

"I was thinking I should get you a dog. Something large and fierce that will guard the house — and you!"

"A dog? I need a dog like a hole in the head," she laughed.

"You spend a lot of time alone and a dog would be a companion. You could take it for walks in the woods."

"And I'd probably leave the door unlocked while I was exercising it."

"Well — think about it," he said. "I'd feel happier knowing you had a protector."

"It's a nice thought, Adam, and please don't think I'm not grateful for your concern, but if this business really does get off the ground, I'll be too busy to look after a pet. Besides, I go away a lot, to visit my parents." She smiled apologetically. She really hoped she hadn't hurt his feelings, but she also wished he wouldn't fuss so much.

"I'd better unpack my shopping," she said, turning to the bags on the counter top.

"I really fancy getting fish and chips. What do you think?"

"Actually, now you mention it, that does sound wonderful." She put the groceries away and followed him outside.

"I know an excellent chip shop near the beach," he told her. "And I've got a bottle of wine in the car — everything we need for a picnic on the beach."

"You actually planned all this, didn't you?"

"Well yes . . ." he confessed. "It seemed like a better plan than that noisy club we spoke of."

"It does sound like a good idea," Sophie agreed.

They drove for about five miles before he turned off the main road and went down to a small cove. The chip shop was crowded, a testimony to its reputation.

"This smell is positive torture," Sophie murmured as they stood in the queue. "I hadn't realised how hungry I was."

They took their steaming hot packages down to the beach and sat on a rug Adam had brought. The sun was setting over the sea, leaving dancing orange trails across the water.

"This was such a good idea, Adam. This fish is amazing."

"Fish and chips always taste better out-doors, preferably by the sea," he said. Then, eyeing her glass, he added, "I see someone's drunk all your wine again."

"How posh is it to have wine with fish and chips?"

"Why not? It's good food and deserves good wine."

"I like your thinking." She smiled.

"Well, I hope you'll like some of the rest

of my thinking," he began. "I met a few people at the conference who'll be able to help us in our future projects."

"Really? Such as?"

"Various media contacts, people I've known for a while." He shrugged. "Some I met at university who have made some progress in their careers. There's one — a photographer who has a growing reputation — she's offered to come and do professional photo-shoots. It'll look great in the bro-chures."

"Hold on," Sophie said warily. "Bro-chures? What exactly do you have in mind?"

"I think we need something glossy to at-tract wealthier clients. Good pictures of some of your most striking outfits to make people really want to be there."

"This sounds extremely expensive, Adam — I was thinking more along the lines of flyers." Her anxiety came to the fore again and she went on, "Look, I've made it clear I don't have much money and I will not get into debt over this. Besides, what if I'm not good enough to put on a whole show — suppose it's all a colossal flop?"

"You've heard of speculate to accumulate? You have to think big and forget about money. I've got heaps, anyway."

"Oh, no," Sophie warned. "I'm not letting

you pay for everything and possibly lose a lot of money over it."

"Look, let me look after the financial side of things," Adam tried to soothe her. "And I'll claim my money back when you're a huge success."

"And if I'm not?"

"Then I'll have lost money I can afford to lose." He shrugged.

"Why, Adam? What makes you so confident in me?"

"I've seen what you can do, Sophie. With just a little bit of backing and encouragement, you've put together a whole string of wedding outfits that would have cost thousands of pounds. And you've made the whole lot in virtually no time at all."

He put his hand on her arm and smiled. "I'm amazed, and I know Chloe is absolutely thrilled with everything. You are going to be a star, Sophie James, I know it."

He took a sip of wine and then continued, "Oh yes, I just remembered — I haven't shown you my latest website design. I suppose I should have really, before I ordered the labels."

"You've ordered labels? What sort of labels?"

"Ones to stitch inside the clothes and then ones to hang from . . . well, wherever it is you hang labels on clothes.

He shrugged and went on to justify himself with, "I asked my photographer friend what she thought and she said she knew someone who would make them in a hurry — after all, you'll want them to sew into the wedding outfits, won't you?"

"I hadn't thought about it, really — everyone knows this is almost a sort of family thing."

"All the same. It doesn't do any harm to look as professional as possible."

"I do think you should have shown me first," she pouted. "We hadn't even decided on the name yet."

"You said you liked just Sophie, so the swing labels say 'Design by Sophie'. I'm sure you'll love them. The printing is in green, to match your eyes."

Sophie finished her wine and remained silent. Though she knew he was doing it all for her sake, she felt that Adam was taking over. He shouldn't have commissioned labels to be printed without even asking her! It was too much.

"Have I upset you?"

"Well, you are taking over a bit. What if I don't like your designs for my labels? You've probably ordered masses."

"It was cheaper to place a large order," he

told her sheepishly. "I pulled in a few favours to get a rush job. I thought you'd be thrilled. I thought you'd see it as the real beginnings of your new career. I'm sorry if I got it wrong . . ."

"It's just that I feel you're pushing me too much." Sophie couldn't help wondering if she was being too cruel but, damn it, she was angry! "I thought we'd agreed that you'd slow down?"

"I thought the no-strings thing was just our relationship. This is business."

"It seems to me that you're pulling all the strings like some demented puppeteer!"

"Well I'm sorry if you're cross!" He frowned and his lovely blue eyes clouded over. "I thought I was doing a good thing," he snapped as he cleared the remnants of their picnic.

"Let's go home now. It's getting chilly now, anyway — and I don't just mean the weather."

Sophie was beginning to feel ashamed; she must have sounded petulant and childish but she had to stick to her guns and she would not be tied to him by debt. He may have plenty of money at his disposal but she was not going to be bought!

In spite of her anger, she was intrigued to know what his labels were like; Chloe had said he was good at that sort of thing. As she watched him shake the sand from the rug and stride back to the car, she wondered why she had spoiled what had been a lovely evening.

It had been a tense journey back as they drove home in silence and when they arrived at her cottage, she was anxious to build bridges if she could. "Will you come in for a coffee?"

"If you still want to spend time with me."

"Of course I do, Adam. I know you were only trying to do something nice for me," she said with a sigh. "But suppose I don't like them after you've spent all that money on them? This is my future and it's important to me that I get everything just right, just what I want it to be."

Adam's face lit up. "I understand that," he conceded, "but I just know you'll love them. I'll bring my laptop in and you can take a look."

She couldn't help but smile at his enthusiasm. "Don't you ever go anywhere without your laptop?"

"Not often."

He bounded back to the car to retrieve his computer and when he came back he suddenly remembered, "Damn, I never did bring my old laptop for you, did I?"

"There's plenty of time, Adam," she told him gently.

They went inside and he immediately switched the computer on. "Right, let's get this over with," he said. "If you don't like it I can cancel the rest of the order immediately."

"The rest?"

"I asked for a couple of dozen as samples to be sent immediately, but the rest will follow later. There it is."

He stood back and watched her expression as she stared at the silver strip bearing the words as he had described. It was classy, discreet and exactly what she would have chosen.

"The swing labels are on the next page." He clicked and a circular shape appeared with the same words: Design by Sophie. "So . . . what do you think . . . ?"

She tried to keep her face straight but could only manage to do so for a few seconds before a grin broke out.

"I love it, Adam! It's just right. I was so afraid you'd go over the top and I'd hate it."

"Surely you realise I have excellent taste?" he grinned back. "Just look at the company I keep for a start."

"Okay, I'm sorry," she told him quietly,

but then she pointed a teasing finger at him and added brightly, "But you must let me see everything before you go commissioning orders. And you must keep account of what you're spending — the dress bags, these labels — everything."

"Call them a present. I never bought you a birthday present, did I?"

"You've no idea when my birthday is. Anyway, we hadn't even met then."

"So there you are, then." He grinned at her boyishly. "All these years of birthdays and I've never bought you a present."

"Don't be a fool!" She laughed but added seriously, "It's very generous of you — but it has to stop there. Thank you, but from now on, the bills come to me."

"Phew, you've got quite a temper, haven't you?"

"I didn't mean to get cross, but this is my business and though I'm grateful for all your help, I don't want you taking over and making decisions that should be mine."

"Okay, got it." He made a mock salute. "But please understand, I was only trying to help and I got this chance to get the labels made and printed at a fraction of what they'd otherwise cost. And I hurried them so you could sew the labels into the wedding outfits. The more exposure you get, the better."

"Okay, thanks for that. But you know my rules now. Everything has to be included in the costs of each design and that includes the labels, packaging, the lot."

"All right and I won't interfere from now on. But once the wedding's over, we do need to complete the website and make definite plans for the show." He held his hand up and Sophie smiled. "Okay, okay, I'm not trying to take over."

"I'll put the coffee on," she said. "And yes, you're right, I do need to get a move on. I'm brimming over with ideas and now I've got these wedding outfits as a centrepiece, I actually believe I can do it. I'm planning mother-of-the-bride outfits as well.

Again, she became quite animated as she went on, "I want various sections to the show. Beachwear of course will be essential as this is Cornwall, and I thought I'd do some fifties looks using the recycled stuff and . . . oh, loads of things."

"When have you been working on these ideas?"

"Sewing long lengths of frills for little dresses and sewing on buttons are all pretty mindless tasks, but the brain runs on."

"It's going to be a huge success, Sophie, I know it. I'm so pleased to see that look on your face again."

"This wedding is a pretty big deal, not least because it's bringing in a decent amount of money."

They sat together on her small sofa as they drank coffee, both of them pleased that good humour seemed to be restored.

"I'd better go now and let you get some rest," Adam said.

Sophie rose from the sofa with him and took a deep breath before she said, "I hate it when we disagree, Adam. Let's make sure it doesn't happen again. And I am very grateful to you for organising the labels."

"I think I'm clear about what I can do and what's not allowed, although . . ." he smiled and turned to her. "Am I allowed a kiss for good behaviour?"

She laughed softly. "I'm not sure about the good behaviour, but you can kiss me because I'd like you to."

She sensed that he was holding back, somehow, holding himself in check as if he knew that things might go much further if he didn't. She felt it too, but she also knew this was still not the right time, she wasn't ready yet, although . . .

"When can I see you again?" he asked.

"I really need to work pretty solidly tomorrow," she told him. "And Rachel and

144

Chloe are coming on Monday for her fitting and I have to make my own dress from scratch if I'm going to do it."

"Tuesday, then? I don't think I can manage much longer than that before seeing you again."

She nodded, knowing in her heart of hearts that she felt exactly the same and that Tuesday couldn't come soon enough.

As she went back inside, she even remembered to lock her door. But later, as she was falling asleep, she heard the roar of motorbikes once more, but she was simply too exhausted to do anything other than murmur, "What on earth are they doing at this time of night?" before she fell asleep.

CHAPTER 9

Sophie looked outside first thing next morning. The tracks from the bikers could be clearly seen, carving deep grooves in the pathways. Outside her cottage, it looked as if someone had been ploughing the ground. She wondered if she should phone the police, or at least let her landlord know what was going on. Such vandalism. It did make her realise she needed to be much more careful about her security.

It seemed impossible to think that only a

week ago, she was swimming in Adam's pool at Rayman's Creek, before Bee was rushed off to the hospital.

Even more impossible to absorb was the few short weeks since she had become involved with Adam and his family.

She had accomplished a lot in the time but if "Design by Sophie" was to be a success, she had to make up her garments in an even shorter time.

She took Rachel's dress as far as she could without a fitting before beginning work on her own. It was so much easier since she knew her own shape so well.

She wasn't quite as slender as Rachel and needed a few subtle changes to make the dresses look the same, but by evening, she was finished.

She was apprehensive about tomorrow, not least because they would tell Rachel that she was also to be a matron of honour. She knew that everything would be wrong with Rachel's dress anyway, and the news would only make matters even worse. Thank goodness Chloe was coming too.

The two were expected at six-thirty. Sophie had tidied the workroom and had everything ready for the fitting when Adam phoned to wish her luck.

"I know you're not looking forward to it,

but I'm sure it will be fine. I'll call you later to see how it went."

"Thanks. I must admit, it's not going to be an easy evening and I'm not looking forward to it."

"You'll be fine. Don't stand any nonsense. In fact, if you're rude enough, she might even fly into a rage and walk out!"

"Now there's a thought. Just don't tempt me too much." Just then Sophie heard a car approach. "Oh, they're here. Thanks again for ringing."

"Good luck," Adam said before she hung up and went to open the door for the two women.

"You must be sick of the sight of blue fabric," Chloe said as they went up the stairs. "And you must be worn out."

"Not at all," Sophie replied. "I love what I do. Now, Rachel, the top is finished apart from the final fastenings at the back. I need to fit it carefully to you so I'll be using some pins to get the lines exactly right."

"Just don't stab me. Blood and scars all over my back would not be a good look," Rachel snapped.

"Well, I managed fine with the little ones so I'm sure you'll be all right." She eased the dress over Rachel's head and let the draped skirt fall gently to the ground. It was a perfect fit and she was delighted with the way it looked.

"Of course it's much too long," Rachel began.

"I haven't done the bottom hem yet. I need to do that after I've fitted you. Did you bring the shoes you'll be wearing?"

"No. Was I supposed to?"

"My fault, I didn't tell you to bring them," Sophie said generously. "Do you know what height will your heels be?"

"Quite high . . . four, five inches."

Sophie glanced at Chloe and raised her eyebrows.

"Not that high," Chloe said. "We haven't been shoe shopping yet, I'm afraid. I was waiting to see if . . ." She tailed off.

She had been about to say something about Sophie being an extra matron of honour. "You look gorgeous, Rachel. You've made a great job of it, Sophie. Well done."

"It isn't quite as bad as I'd expected," Rachel conceded somewhat ungraciously. "So, what's that other thing on your dressmaker's dummy?"

Sophie looked anxiously at Chloe.

This was surely the time to break the news, but Sophie wanted Chloe to be the one to tell her?

She took the hint. "Actually Rachel, I've

asked Sophie to be a matron of honour, too," Chloe said briskly, as if she wanted to get it over with as quickly as possible. "You're about the same height and I thought it would make things more symmetrical. Besides, I wanted her to be a part of my day, especially since she's done such a fantastic job on the dresses."

"You are kidding me?" Rachel snapped. "So how does that work with the best man?"

"Sorry?"

"Well, traditionally the matron of honour is partnered with the best man for the day."

"Well, Sophie and Adam are together anyway, so it seemed another good reason to include her. There are two or three ushers. You can take your pick," Chloe said and briskly moved on with, "Now, about the shoes. I thought we might meet in Truro tomorrow and buy a couple of matching pairs. Can you do that, both of you?"

"Not sure," Rachel said, snippily, her voice still registering her anger on a very high level.

"Okay, well if Sophie and I go and choose something, you can go and try them later, when you do have time."

"But I need input on what's selected. She'd undoubtedly choose something frumpy, as I very much doubt that Sophie and I share a taste in anything. Why don't I choose the shoes and Sophie can go and collect hers?"

Rachel didn't even try to hide her irritation as she continued her rant. "This is all turning into a total shambles, if you ask me. If you wanted her to be your matron of honour, why did you bother to ask me in the first place?"

"Actually Rachel, if you recall, it was you who insisted on it — and you made it impossible for me to say no."

"That's not how I remember it." Rachel sniffed. "I seem to recall something about you hoping all those wretched little girls would behave themselves. You practically begged me to come and take charge for you."

The normally placid Chloe finally lost her temper. "What planet are you on, Rachel? When you heard Adam was to be best man, you fell over yourself to get me to agree! Whatever it was then, this is how things are now, and if you want to opt out, that's fine by me. So, are you going to meet us tomorrow or not? It's my last chance. I'm busy for the rest of the week."

Angrily and reluctantly, and after a great deal of fuss, Rachel finally agreed to meet them the following day.

Sophie unpinned the dress and marked the placing of the fastenings. They had decided that they'd choose heels about the same height as the ones Rachel was wearing, so she marked the hem and could finish the dress without needing to see Rachel again before the day. That was some relief, at least.

"Oh! I got the dolls too," Chloe said. "I'll get them from the car. The girls will be thrilled."

"I must say, you seem remarkably in control," Sophie told Chloe. "Considering you're moving to New York just a few days after the wedding. With all that on top, I'd be a gibbering wreck by now, I'm sure."

"Oh, I think I'm getting close," she muttered, casting her eyes upwards to where Rachel was still getting dressed. "If I hear one more time how she stepped into the breach as a favour to me, I shall throw up!"

When Rachel finally came downstairs, she glanced round to make sure that Chloe was absent.

"Don't think you've won, you little bitch! I'll get Adam in the end. You do realise he's way out of your class? He's only after you for one thing anyway, and when he's had enough, you'll be tossed on one side like all the rest of his conquests."

She sneered at Sophie, who was stunned speechless. "And don't think I haven't seen you taking him up to your bedroom. And if you persist in chasing him, I'll make sure you're sorry you ever met him."

Chloe returned just as she'd finished her vitriolic speech and Rachel smiled sweetly as if nothing had happened.

"Can I offer you anything to drink?" Sophie was digging her fingernails into her hands to stop herself from exploding.

"I need to get back, but thanks anyway," Chloe said, unaware of what had gone on between the other two women. "Thanks again for everything. And I'll bring my cheque book with me tomorrow if you can let me know how much I owe you."

"Thanks very much. I'll work out a final bill for you."

"Make sure you include everything, won't you? No leaving this or that off the total. And of course you must include the cost of your own dress, too."

"You're very kind, thank you." She showed them out and saw Adam sitting in his car parked outside. He climbed out and greeted the two women.

"Why didn't you come in?" Chloe asked.

"What and get tangled up in all that girlie stuff? No thanks, I'm not that brave. I came with supper for the worker. Do you know, she never eats unless I feed her?"

"Adam, darling. You're spoiling her." Rachel sniffed haughtily. "You're just too kind-hearted, bringing food parcels for the poor of the parish. I could always stay on and then you could take me home afterwards. Your place or mine, I don't mind . . ."

Adam glowered at Rachel and Chloe simply stared, astounded at the depths of the woman's self-deception.

"Come on, Rachel, leave them in peace," she said, practically dragging Rachel away. "See you next week, Adam. I hope you're not planning anything too extreme for the stag night on Friday."

"Not at all. How about the hen night? I bet you'll be much more lively than us!"

"I haven't even thought about it. I don't think I'll bother — I have too much to do. Come on Rachel."

"How did it go?" Adam asked as soon as they'd driven off.

"It could have been worse, I suppose, though not much." She was too angry to say anything else and breathed deeply to calm her rising temper. "Come on in."

"I've brought fresh-baked Cornish pasties and a bowl of mixed salad. What could be better than that?" he said.

"You really do intend me to be as fat as butter, don't you?"

As they ate, Sophie calmed down enough to tell Adam what Rachel had said when Chloe wasn't there. They even managed to laugh over Rachel's remarks and Sophie realised it was a relief to have it out in the open and talk to Adam about it.

"It was horrible, she was so threatening. And she must have followed you, Adam — she quite openly said she saw the upstairs light on and assumed it was a typical bedroom scenario." She could feel her anger mounting again.

"Let's forget about her, Sophie. I've had enough of Rachel." Adam frowned. By the way, did the labels arrive?"

"No. Actually, I didn't hear the post come at all today." Sophie got up and went out to her postbox and returned clutching a package. "They were here all the time. I'm sorry, I was so busy I forgot to look."

Her fingers trembled slightly as she tore off the wrapping. "Oh, wow! Oh, Adam, they're gorgeous!" She felt really quite emotional as she saw the first sign of her business finally becoming official. "I must send one to my mum and dad. They'll be so thrilled."

"You don't mention your parents very

often," Adam observed. "Where do they live?"

"Near Bristol."

"Don't you see them much?"

"Not really. They're very involved with their own projects. My mother's a painter and Dad is always busy organising his youngsters. They have a sort of smallholding where disabled young folk come to work each day. You know, a sort of broadening experience for people who need day care."

"It sounds wonderful — and very worthwhile."

"They never have two beans to rub together but they're happy. I always call them my ageing hippies."

Adam smiled. "I'd love to meet them some day."

Sophie frowned. It wasn't that she was ashamed of her parents, but they were so different to anyone Adam could possibly know.

Perhaps it was just that she wasn't secure in knowing where she and Adam were headed in the future. Listening to his words, she could almost believe that his mind was fully made up and he saw his future with her, but she worried that he could just be swept along by their shared enthusiasm for a new project.

Was this how Adam always behaved? Was he always such an enthusiastic person? She had the feeling he might be.

But deep down, everything told her that she still needed to be very cautious before she made any big commitment to him.

"Why the frown?" Adam observed. "Is there something wrong with your parents?"

"Of course not, they're great." She shrugged. "I just wouldn't have thought they were your sort of people, though."

"And what exactly are my sort of people?"

"Well, Chloe and your cousin and all your wealthy relations. You own a business with offices in foreign places I don't even know about."

"But family is family, and not the friends I choose to spend my time with."

"You don't seem to spend much time with them, judging by the amount of time you've given to me in the past weeks."

"Only because I've chosen to. I've had a couple of nights out with friends. I played squash one night last week and went out for a drink afterwards. I consider getting to know you properly is my priority at the moment. The more time we can spend together, the better we'll know each other when we need to make decisions about our future."

"That sounds a bit serious." Sophie tried

not to let herself get carried away with false hopes. "I'm sure you'll meet my parents at some point. Maybe they'll come to the fashion show. After all, it's a pretty big deal for their one and only child."

"Well, I'm glad you like the labels, but I suppose I'd better go now and let you get on. We've both got a busy few days ahead. I'll see you later in the week."

He rose to leave. "Oh, and you really should organise something for Chloe's hen night. I'll have a word with Bee and see if she can give us a list of her friends and we'll keep it quiet from Rachel. You'd do that, wouldn't you? Even if it's just drinks in a wine bar or something?"

"I'd be happy to — I like Chloe."

His goodbye kiss seemed to linger on her lips for some time after he left.

Could it really be that they had a future together? Only time would tell, she supposed.

She pushed Rachel's threats out of her mind as the empty taunts of a jealous woman. She had so much work to get through in such a short space of time; she couldn't afford to let Rachel get to her.

The rest of the week passed quickly. Everything had gone far too smoothly, Sophie was thinking. What had she forgotten?

They had spent a pleasant evening in a wine bar on Friday evening, and Chloe had invited some of her colleagues from work and said goodbye to them all.

Sophie had heard nothing from Adam about the stag night and it was Sunday before he called her.

"I wondered what your plans are for tomorrow night, before the wedding? Most of the party are staying at the hotel. I expect you have to take the dresses over, ready for the big day?"

"I hadn't discussed it with Chloe. I assumed I'd take them on Tuesday morning, straight to the hotel. I suppose I'll have to find some way of transporting them. My car won't hold them."

"I'll borrow Dad's people carrier," Adam reassured her. "Shall I book a room for you at the hotel? It would be easier if you're on hand, wouldn't it?"

Sophie frowned. The hotel where the wedding was being held was a huge place, with huge charges to match. She didn't really want to pay out such a lot just for one night.

As if he'd read her mind, Adam added, "If it's the cost you're thinking about, we've got a bulk deal, an all-in package. It's just a matter of letting them know how many rooms to prepare."

"Well, if you're sure . . . it would save a lot of hassle."

"Great! I'll come over tomorrow morning with Dad's car and we can load everything in and make just one journey," he said, pleased with himself. "I'll have to leave you to it after that to get on with my best man duties. There's going to be a pre-wedding dinner at the hotel on Monday night and then we move to the different wings so the bride and groom don't run into each other again before the ceremony."

"So I'll need something smart for the dinner, then?"

"Reasonably. I'm sure you'll find something in your remarkable collection. Oh and I've had a few business cards printed for you — just in case anyone asks, you never know," Adam ventured carefully. "They're the same colours as the labels with the same logo and your phone number. Don't be cross with me," he added quickly. "I know what you said about me taking over but I knew you wouldn't have time. I did wonder if we should put them out on the tables but I decided you might not like that . . ."

"I wouldn't ever have thought about cards," Sophie said. She could tell he was trying so hard not to upset her and she felt a little guilty; after all, he was only trying to help. "Thank you, Adam, that's a great idea. Gosh, this could be almost as important as my first show."

After she'd said goodbye to Adam, she spent the rest of the day checking and pressing everything.

She packed up an emergency sewing kit and finally put together her own things for the dinner and overnight stay. There was a hairdresser and make-up artist coming to the hotel for the morning. She even remembered to pack a roll of wrapping paper for the dolls, in case Chloe wanted it.

Adam made sure that Sophie felt a part of everything at the family dinner. She had confessed earlier that she felt a bit of an interloper but Chloe's family were full of praise for the work she had done. They had been to inspect everything and were delighted with the bridal clothes.

She had to admit to herself that she had been thrilled when she had sewn in her labels, giving them the final touch that made them her exclusive designs. Even Rachel had been forced to concede that her dress was acceptable. Sophie was probably more nervous than the bride herself!

Most new wives say that their wedding

day passed in a flash and that they needed the photographs to remind them of all the different events and the people that were present. Although she wasn't the bride, Sophie felt much the same way.

But when she looked at the photographs later, she would remember the fun they'd had dressing the excited little girls in their pretty dresses and the joy of seeing her own creations truly come to life.

She had received many enquiries and Adam had made sure she handed out the business cards.

His own role had been carried out with great assurance and his best man speech was wonderful; full of humour and perfect for the occasion.

It had been a magical day.

When it was all finally over, Sophie was exhausted, even though it had finished early because of the children. Adam drove her home in the evening and when they arrived at her cottage, tired but happy, she told him, "I'm glad it finished early. I couldn't have lasted if they'd had a disco late into the night."

"I agree," Adam replied. "Though it might have been nice to dance with you again. At least Rachel sort of behaved herself."

"Apart from hissing at me whenever we

were on our own. She's threatened me with all sorts if I don't let you go."

"You're kidding me?" Adam gasped. "But she can't behave like that. I'll have to sort this out once and for all."

"It's okay, Adam. She's just a poor delusional woman. You're here with me, aren't you? Perhaps it's best just to leave it — I'm sure she'll get fed up eventually and go away."

"Okay. If you say so," Adam said doubtfully. "You know, we should go to that club one evening, now that the pressure's off."

"I suspect a whole new lot of pressure is just about to start, what with the fashion show." Spontaneously, she added, "Thanks for everything, Adam. You've totally changed my life."

Adam smiled softly. "I'm glad. I have a feeling both our lives are going to change after this. Next stop, Fashion Show. I'd suggest we take some well-deserved time off until the weekend and then we can start planning in earnest. I can bring the wedding outfits back here to store until the show."

"Oh, I don't suppose you have anywhere to keep them, have you?" Sophie suddenly thought. "Only I need space for the next lot of work. Mind you, they might need cleaning, so I'd better take a look at them."

"I can keep them in my spare room," Adam offered. "Actually, storage space is something we'll have to think of in future."

"Right now all I can think of is that I feel as if I could sleep for a week." Sophie tried to stifle a yawn.

"And I have to go into work tomorrow morning as well as somehow find time to go back to the hotel and collect and return all the suits and things, so I'd better be going."

"Goodnight Adam. And thank you again."

"Good night, Sophie, darling," Adam murmured. "And . . . don't be upset, but . . . I prefer the natural you, not all this professional make-up and stiffly sprayed hair." He touched his fingertips to her cheek. "I like the inner Sophie best."

"Oh, Adam." Sophie laughed softly. "You're such a fool."

But her cottage felt empty and too quiet once he'd gone. She made some hot chocolate after she'd cleaned off the professional make-up, as Adam had called it, and brushed out the hair spray. The "inner Sophie" was revealed again.

Suddenly her thoughts brought her up short. He had called her darling . . . and what's more, she realised, she had really rather liked it.

CHAPTER 10

There was a huge sense of anti-climax the next day. Sophie wandered round the cottage doing ordinary things like cleaning and laundry before she tidied the workroom. Adam was right; storage was going to be a major problem. Perhaps she needed to rent somewhere — but it was a major move forward and something she couldn't afford at this stage.

But if she wanted to have a proper business, she needed a studio and workshop. Her upstairs room was adequate for small projects, but for a full-blown fashion show? The wedding outfits had filled a whole rail on their own.

The sun was shining and the woods were calling. She hadn't been for a walk in ages and she needed to clear her head and take time to think.

If she rented a studio, it would mean daily travelling, something she had not missed at all over the past weeks. Perhaps she should think of moving house? She would miss all this, she thought as she watched rabbits and squirrels dashing about their business.

Looking out at the views from the wedding venue had reminded her of her other love that she had been neglecting: the sea.

She deserved a whole day off. She would go back to the cottage, collect her car and drive to the coast.

Still pondering the future, she wandered along the cliffs enjoying the impact of the colours. The sea was a brilliant blue and the cliffs were lined with the pink thrift that embellished them each spring. Golden gorse, almost too bright to look at in the sunshine, filled the air with a scent reminiscent of coconut.

The thought of moving anywhere outside Cornwall did not appeal one little bit.

Perhaps she should go to see her parents, discuss things with them. They had managed to find happiness away from Cornwall, despite their earlier doubts. When they had decided to leave the somewhat primitive chalet that had been home during her early years, it had been a difficult time.

The death of her grandparents had provided them with the means to buy a piece of land and a near-derelict cottage in Somerset, some miles outside Bristol. She had been at university in Cornwall, so she had stayed.

They had helped her with rent to begin with, but they soon needed every spare penny to begin their own projects.

She had taken on various temporary jobs to pay her way and now it looked as if her own ambitions were finally about to be realised at last.

She looked at her watch; it was almost four. Her parents would be finishing their day, so she pulled out her mobile and dialled their number.

"Hi, Mum, are you busy?'

"Sophie! I haven't heard from you in ages. Is everything all right, love?"

"Everything's great, Mum," she said, though she knew her voice sounded far from it. "I've so much to tell you. Can I come and see you?"

"When were you thinking of?"

"Now? I can drive up and be with you in say, three hours?"

"Are you sure there's nothing wrong?"

"Far from it. I've got heaps of news."

"All right. Dad's got a meeting in the village this evening but it won't be a late one. I'll put some extra vegetables in the pot."

Sophie almost ran back to the car, drove to the cottage and packed up her overnight things. She even remembered to lock the door this time, which was more than she had done earlier. At least Adam hadn't called to tell her off.

Adam. She had better let him know she was going away or he'd panic if he couldn't get hold of her. Though he'd said he'd leave her until the weekend, he might decide to just turn up, as he often did. She sent a text to his mobile. He would still be busy working, but by the time he finished she would be driving and unable to answer her phone.

The roads were fairly clear and she was soon passing Exeter and onto the M5. Just after seven o'clock she pulled up outside her parents' home, where two Jack Russell terriers ran out to greet her, barking noisily, followed by her mother.

"Hello, darling. You look tired, but very well — blooming, in fact — but a bit tired round the eyes."

"Life's been a bit hectic lately. Oh, I've got a bottle of wine in the car, hang on . . ." She pulled out the bottle and her bag and followed her mother into the house.

The place was as untidy as ever and smelt of something delicious cooking in the oven. The cosy kitchen was cluttered with animal beds, and stacks of freshly picked vegetables lay on every surface and herbs were strung on high racks drying. The table had heaps of papers and several books lying open and just two spaces left empty for her parents to eat.

What a contrast it all was from the super-efficient kitchen at Adam's place!

"So why is life suddenly so hectic for you?"

"Perhaps I should wait until Dad gets home — if he's not going to be too late, that is?"

"He should be back by eight. It's a meeting about some planning issue that has the village up in arms, but he knows you're coming. How about a cuppa?"

"Lovely, Mum. What's cooking? It smells wonderful."

"Just a stew, with lots of our own herbs and vegetables."

"So, what's been happening, Mum? Tell me all your news."

"Actually, we're a bit worried that we're about to lose some of our clients. They're cutting back on day care provision in the County. Wretched government economies. The youngsters will miss it all so much and we don't know what else we're going to do to make up the shortfall."

"I'm so sorry, Mum. You've worked so hard to build this place up. But what about your paintings?"

"Folks tend not to buy stuff like that when the economy is in meltdown," her mother replied gently.

Sophie suddenly felt guilty. She had been so wound up in her own affairs, she hadn't even registered that the cutbacks could affect her parents so directly.

"But I expect we'll manage somehow," her mother added. "We usually manage to find a way — but if you know the odd millionaire who might like to make a few donations to some worthwhile youth projects, we'd be very pleased."

Sophie managed a feeble smile. She possibly did know an odd millionaire, but instead she said, "When I make my first million, you'll be top of my list. Mind you, you might be too old to want it by then . . . is that Dad I can hear?"

"Hello love," he called out. "We're honoured — it's not often you grace us with your presence. Hope there's nothing wrong."

'Why do you always think there's something wrong if I come to see you? It's all good news from my side, but I'm sorry to hear of your problems."

"I'll get supper on the table," her mother said. "Do you want to open the wine, love? Sophie brought it."

"Temping must be paying better than I

thought. This is a decent bottle," her father said.

"She says she's going to tell us her news once we're sitting down; I've had to wait till you got here before she'd say a word. Mind you, from the look on her face, I suspect she's met a man." Her mother leaned over and grabbed her hand, inspecting the ring finger. "Nothing official yet, then?"

"Mum! There are other things in life than getting married," she giggled, although lately it seemed the only things in her life was someone or other getting married. She reached for her handbag and took out the labels and business cards.

"This is my news," she said, smiling.

"Oh, my goodness! You're designing properly? How wonderful!" her mother said.

"Well done, lass," her father added. "Well, you'd better tell us the whole story, then."

During the meal she told them all the details of the wedding, meeting Adam and the planned fashion show.

"So this Adam," her mother said. "How did you meet him?"

"At my last temping job."

"And you like him?"

"Yes, actually, I like him a lot."

"But he's not so keen?"

"Just the opposite really. But after Sam, I

daren't get too involved, Mum. It isn't long since we met so there's no hurry."

"But he's helping you with your business, lass?"

"Well yes, I suppose so. He certainly gets things done and he knows an awful lot of people. I just have to stop him taking over completely," Sophie replied.

"So when do we get to meet him?"

The questions went on until bedtime and, without giving too much away about his family and business, she seemed to manage to satisfy her parents. Looking round, she knew that Adam would never fit in with all of this. For her it was a cosy home but for Adam, it would be chaos.

"I'd better go and check on the animals," her father said. "Come on, dogs. You can chase off any foxes lurking around."

"I'm so proud of you, love," her mother said warmly. "You're doing what you always wanted to do. Even your dollies were the best dressed in the country."

"Thanks Mum. I was going to ask your advice about a few things but I don't want to bother you when you've clearly got troubles of your own,"

"We're all right, dear. We'll come through it eventually, but it's our youngsters that concern me. They're making such progress, some of them, and now it'll all stop. Anyway, you need to get to bed now. We'll talk in the morning, love."

Sophie lay awake for a long time, thinking of the way her parents lived and what they had achieved.

It wasn't on the same scale as Adam's parents but she wondered if the Gilberts were truly as happy and content as her own parents? Her mum and dad had a wonderful relationship and shared so many ideals. They may not be perfect but she loved them dearly and resolved to see more of them in future.

When morning finally came, they had a leisurely breakfast, with sausages from the local butcher in the village and eggs from their own hens.

"Do you always eat like this in a morning?" she asked. "Mind you, Adam's been feeding me up a lot over the past few weeks."

"You talk a lot about this Adam," her father said. "Just be careful won't you, love? He doesn't sound like one of us."

"I don't think he is. But I am being careful. I promise."

"What was the advice you were going to ask?" her mother reminded her.

"I'm trying to decide whether I should rent some sort of studio and workshop. I've got savings but I feel I need to keep some back for emergencies."

"Good heavens, you don't take after your father, do you?" Mrs James laughed. "He doesn't know the meaning of saving."

"If I do take on a place, it would mean I'd have to travel every day and that's much less convenient. Ideally I could do with a place that would do both home and work-shop but then I'd miss my lovely peaceful little corner of the woods . . . despite the recent influx of some biker gang . . ."

"Bikers? Oh, please take care and make sure you lock up," her mother pleaded. "But you know this is something only you can decide. I'm flattered you came all this way to talk it through but we can't be any help. We haven't got anything spare at the moment and our own future is looking a bit murky."

"Oh no, Mum. I wasn't after a loan or anything. I think I just needed to talk it through."

"So what does your Adam think about it all, then?"

"He's not 'my Adam' and we haven't talked about it. He'd probably offer to pay for it and I don't want that."

"He's got money then, has he?"

"Well, yes, but I want to be independent,"

she answered.

"I'm sure you'll make the right decision, but I would take what help anyone wants to offer if it means you'll get where you want to be." Her father leaned back in his chair.

"But if things don't work out, I'd be in such a mess."

"You need to think it all through carefully, love," her mother said. "Follow your head and not your heart."

"Like we did, you mean?" Mr James teased.

"Well you surely don't want her to end up living in a pathetic little chalet half her life, like we did?"

"Actually, I enjoyed living there, practically on the beach." Sophie smiled at the memory of her first home.

"That wasn't what you said in the middle of winter when there were howling gales." Her mother laughed.

A whole flood of "do you remember?" conversation followed until her father heard a vehicle approaching.

"Heavens, it can't be that time already? I'll have to go out and see the gang get started. See you later."

"I think I'll leave you to it now, Mum, and get back to Cornwall," Sophie suggested. "I have a lot to think about, but it's been lovely seeing you and I promise I won't leave it so long next time. And I'll send you invitations to the show. You'll try to come, won't you?"

"You know your dad, love, but if he can't come, I'll try to get there somehow."

"I hope you don't mind if I get back. Just talking it through has really helped put some things into perspective and I hope things work out for you. Keep in touch."

She went to say goodbye to her father and watched him helping a teenage girl to feed the hens. The look of delight on the young woman's face was worth everything. He gave his daughter a wave and blew a kiss.

As she drove back to her cottage, she was even more thoughtful. They may never have had much money but they had achieved something much more. She hoped they would be able to hold on to some of it for the future. Perhaps she should have stayed for longer and spent more time talking.

When she finally parked outside her cottage she sat in her car and stared at it for a long time. Could she bear to leave it? It looked so lovely but her head told her that it was impractical, though her heart was tugging the opposite way.

What she really needed was a large area for a workshop and some sort of flat attached to it. The local paper was out today, so she turned round and drove to the village to buy one.

As she looked through the property adverts, Sophie realized that anything suitable was well out of her price range. Even with the wedding money, her future income would be erratic.

The best she might afford would be some sort of lock-up but that needed to be warm and dry, or clothes would be damaged.

Storing things in Adam's spare room was hardly a long term solution. For now, she just had to make the best of what she had. She went to make some tea and saw the kitchen window had been repaired.

Adam must have organised it, bless him.

For the next two days, she sorted through some of the clothes and planned new outfits that could be made from them. She unpicked things, laundered garments and made numerous drawings. Though she had thought about it before, now she had an incentive to do the work and ideas for the show were coming thick and fast.

True to his word, Adam had left her alone for the week and on Saturday, he arrived early in the morning.

"What's been going on out there? Everywhere's all been messed up," he commented in concern.

"Bikers. They keep using this path as a race track."

"That's awful. I don't like you being out here on your own. Especially if you leave the door unlocked."

"I'm all right. They just seem to ride through the woods."

"Well, all right, Miss-Independent-James. Time to get down to work, then. I've got the wedding stuff in the car for you to examine and see if it needs cleaning. I've brought the old laptop for you to use and I need to know exactly where we're going."

"I see. This is Adam in full organising mode, is it?"

"Sorry. I'm not trying to take over, I just wanted to know what you've been planning this week, what you've been doing."

"I'll make coffee, then. I think we're going to need it."

"I'll unload the car. Straight upstairs?"

"Thanks. Yes, please, there should be just about enough hanging space. I'll decide if they need cleaning later."

Once coffee was made and the wedding clothes hung away, Adam began by showing her how to use the laptop.

"Are you sure you don't need it?" Sophie

asked. "This is practically brand new compared to mine."

"I have another one; I'm afraid I'm a bit of a techno junkie. As long as you can manage the basics, you'll be fine. I want you to be able to access all the information on the Internet more easily; it can save you hours of driving and trudging round the shops."

"Are there any property adverts? I looked at the local paper to see what's around, but couldn't find much. I really need more work space as well as storage."

"I've been thinking the same, actually. Let's see if we can find anything here."

They pored over various websites and advertisements but found nothing suitable.

"Leave it with me for a bit," Adam suggested. "I have some contacts who may know of something. Would you consider somewhere else to live as well?"

"That depends where it is."

"Let me guess. Somewhere peaceful, or by the sea?"

"Ideally — but that probably puts it out of reach financially."

"Okay. I'll see what I can find."

"It seems as if you have contacts everywhere."

"I suppose so," he said. "It's in my line of business and with my background anyway, I know people. Networking and all that — it's something you need to cultivate, Sophie," he suggested.

He looked around and added, "Working in your isolated cottage doesn't get you out there and exposed to the masses, you know. So, tell me what else have you been doing all week?"

"I went to see my parents . . ." she began.

"Oh yes, you sent me a text. That wasn't planned, was it?"

"Impulse. I decided to show them the labels and cards instead of sending them. They were thrilled. I also told them about you and they quizzed me endlessly — and they warned me to let my head do the thinking, not my heart, which is exactly the opposite of their own attitude to life. I'm a bit concerned about them actually . . ."

Adam made no comment and waited for her to tell him about their problems, and when she'd done, he said, "It seems such a shame that something so worthwhile is going to go under. Can anything be done to help them?"

"I don't know, Adam. I tried to lighten things by promising I'd help them out when I've made my first million." She gave a thin smile. "But it might be too late by then."

"So, when do I get to meet them?" Adam asked.

"One day. Like I said, they're not like you and your family."

"If they're anything like you and from what you've said, they sound really lovely. I'm no snob, you know; I'm a bit sad that you are even concerned about that."

"It isn't that; it's just that . . . I mean we . . . well, we as a couple are still very new."

"Hey, wait a minute — was that an admission that we are actually a couple?" Adam's handsome face lit up.

"Well . . . yes . . . no. I mean I'm being your 'and other' so often now, it means we must be some sort of couple, I suppose. But it's just too soon to meet my parents and I'd rather get to know you better . . ."

"And what about my parents? You met them the first time we went anywhere together."

"That was all circumstantial. Meeting my folks takes an actual journey specifically to visit them. Now please, Adam, can we get on with whatever we need to? This is getting us nowhere. What do we need to decide next?"

"Your website," Adam said with a sigh.

Just then the phone rang. Sophie picked it

up but all she heard was a nasty hissing sound.

"What's that?" Adam quizzed her. "Your phone seems to be making an odd noise."

"It keeps happening. I just ignore it now . . . Oh, by the way, thank you for repairing the kitchen window. I'm not sure how you did it without getting in."

"I did it from the outside — not difficult really." Adam looked back to the laptop and added, "We need to book a venue and fix the date next, I think; then when the website goes live, it will all be in place."

"We talked about a charity, before. I'd like something that helps young people with disabilities. That would be in line with my parents' ideas." Sophie stretched her arms and rubbed her temples. "I'm exhausted after all that. All I have to do now is design and make a mass of clothes. Easy!"

"Would you like to do something this evening? There's still the club we were going to check out."

"Do you really like clubs? I have to confess I'm not really into clubbing as a favourite way to spend an evening."

"I have a confession to make — nor am I," Adam said. "What about the cinema? Or theatre?"

"I love them both, but I don't get the

chance to go very often. In fact, I haven't been in years."

"Let's see what's on. I'd enjoy seeing a film for a change."

They decided on a popular costume drama that had good reviews and Adam booked seats using the computer.

"I didn't even realise you could do that," Sophie said, impressed. "It saves queueing, I suppose."

"It's time we dragged you into the twenty-first century!"

They enjoyed the film but Sophie spent most of the time looking at the clothes and gleaning even more ideas.

"What did you think?" Adam asked as they left the cinema.

"I thought the costumes in the second scene at the country house party were really beautiful. It made me think I need to get some ideas for menswear too."

"Sophie!" Adam laughed. "Did you actually see anything of the film or were you just looking at the clothes?"

"Both really." Sophie laughed too. "I doubt I'll ever stop looking at what people are wearing."

They sat in the car outside her cottage for a few minutes. He turned down her invitation for coffee, saying he needed to get home. Sophie was slightly disappointed but realised it was for the best. If she relaxed any more in his company, who could tell what might happen? He was everything she could ever have wanted — so why was she still so intent on being cautious? It made no sense, but something was always holding her back.

"Why so quiet?" Adam asked.

"Sorry, I was still thinking about . . . about the film," she improvised. "Should she have given in to him or held back?"

"And are you talking about the heroine in the film, or maybe about yourself?"

"I don't know what you mean," she protested.

"I'm not stupid, Sophie, but I am prepared to wait till you've sorted things out in your mind, or your heart or whatever it is."

Sophie went inside to her empty home and slumped down on the sofa. It was definitely a night for hot chocolate.

It had been a really great day with Adam and she had enjoyed the film but towards the end of the evening, there had been a distinct chill in the air.

She tried to take comfort from his words; he said he was prepared to wait. But why did she need him to wait — what was holding her back?

She noticed her answering machine was flashing; she pressed the play button and winced as a very loud whistle filled the room, followed by a loud hiss, and some indistinguishable words. Who on earth . . . ? She dialled the number to see who had called but was told the caller had not revealed their identity.

She was getting tired of this and decided to do something tomorrow about screening her calls.

CHAPTER 11

Sunday was a long day at Sophie's cottage. She kept staring at the phone, wondering who had made yet another disturbing call. She thought of Adam's family Sunday with Bee and Dennis and their children, all enjoying lunch together. She had not been invited again.

With a sigh, she picked up her drawing pad and began some sketches, but ideas just kept going round in circles in her mind, so she abandoned her efforts and went out. Maybe some sea air would clear her mind.

She made mental notes as she walked: Somewhere to store clothes, somewhere to work, maybe somewhere to live, a venue for the show . . . organisation. She needed help and a lot of it. Was Adam the right person? After all, he had a responsible job, which he must have been neglecting lately.

She sat on the sea wall and looked around. There were several small shops in this village, and a number of holiday lets. All seaside villages in Cornwall seemed to have a lot of holiday lets, but nothing permanent. She would have to move inland.

She had to get a grip, she told herself; it was time to stop floundering around and get down to business. She must concentrate, stop her speculation about Adam and settle down to work. Full of resolve, she went back to her cottage.

When she got there, the front door was wide open. She felt sure she had locked it and called out as she went inside. Nothing seemed to have been disturbed, but she still felt more than a little uncomfortable.

She opened the fridge to get some milk out, and stared — it was completely empty. She opened the freezer compartment and that was stripped bare, too. Some tramp must have broken in and taken all the food! At least that was replaceable.

Thank goodness the wedding outfits were back at Adam's place. She rushed upstairs in a panic, but her precious clothes hadn't been damaged.

She gave a shudder; she felt violated. What else had been examined, prodded or even stolen? Should she phone the police? It was a bit late, but she knew she could never settle now, so she dialled the number and then went out to walk round the outside of the cottage.

Along one side, a whole box of eggs had been thrown at the walls, presumably the eggs from her fridge. She walked a little way into the woods, not letting her cottage out of sight and she found most of the contents of her fridge and freezer ground into the mud. This was no tramp; this was a vicious attack on her property, something mean and spiteful.

Could it be Rachel's handiwork? Surely not!

Two officers came round eventually and looked somewhat half-heartedly for any clues. She told them that the cottage had been locked but they were sceptical as there was no sign of damage on any doors or windows.

"It was probably kids. I shouldn't worry, Miss, no adult would do something so mindless. We'll make a report and you can let us know if anything else happens."

They looked at the damaged ground. "Have you been troubled with bikers?" Sophie nodded. "We'll have a word. I think that's your answer, though — you probably left your door open and they thought they'd have a bit of fun."

Not greatly reassured, Sophie watched them leave. Tomorrow, she would have to re-stock her food supply and then get back to work.

For two days, she worked in the isolation she normally loved, but now she felt nervous at every sound she heard, her peace was spoiled. Each time her phone rang, she jumped and waited for the answering machine to identify the callers. She heard nothing from Adam until Tuesday evening.

"I've got news," he said in great excitement. "Can I come over?" Despite her resolutions, she couldn't stop her heart giving a little leap of excitement.

She speculated madly about his news while she waited for him. Perhaps he had contacted a charity and they were ready to take part in the fashion show.

When he arrived he launched straight in with, "I've only found you the perfect place to live and work! A friend of mine has converted several outbuildings on a farm outside Truro. They're mostly holiday lets but he has one left and couldn't decide how to use what is potentially a large space. I looked at it last night and I think it would be perfect for you, Sophie! It's a huge open plan room with a small flat above it with one bedroom and open plan living space. It's about four times bigger than your room upstairs. There's a bit to do to finish off, but you'd be able to live and work on site. There's loads of parking and everything — and the rent's not too bad either!"

He finally stopped for breath and looked at her expectantly. "What do you think?"

"It sounds perfect but it depends on how much 'not too bad' actually is." He mentioned a figure that sounded too good to be true. "Really? That's hardly any more than I pay for this place. And truth to be told . . . I've been a bit scared lately . . ." She confessed about the break-in and the phone calls.

"Why on earth didn't you call me?" Adam demanded. "I'd have come over to stay and keep you safe."

Sophie suddenly felt a little weepy but controlled herself. "I didn't want to sound like a helpless female or bother you when you've already helped me so much." She rallied herself and changed the subject. "So tell me about this place you've found. And why is it so cheap?"

"He's prepared to do a deal because we're old friends and his parents are friends of mine; when they retired from the farm he took over. You'll like him, Miles is a really good bloke and his wife Martha's great. We can go and look as soon as you like."

"Oh, Adam, it sounds amazing." But Sophie wondered if she could cope with a move on top of everything else.

Adam's friend lived in a delightful old farm house with a large yard surrounded by the various conversions, all beautifully done and Sophie immediately felt concerned that this was seriously beyond her ability to pay. "Are you certain the price you quoted is for real?" she whispered to Adam.

"Because you'd be a long let, he's reducing the price," he reassured her. "Here he comes . . . Miles, meet Sophie James; Sophie, Miles Turner."

"Sophie, delighted to meet you. I've been hearing wonderful things about you." He gave her an open, friendly smile as he shook her hand warmly. "I hope you'll like the premises. I'd love to have a fashion expert living here — as would my wife! I can imagine she'll be a regular customer!"

Miles was a tall, rather good-looking man, clearly from a similar back ground to Adam, very well-spoken and with a confident manner.

"Thank you," Sophie replied. "It sounds perfect for me."

"It's round here, at the back of the yard. This is why it hasn't been completely finished yet. I couldn't decide how to best use the space as it's no good for holiday lets. Then Adam phoned me yesterday to see how it was going and, bingo. Here it is."

He unlocked the door of what had once been some sort of farm building. It looked vast; a space with nothing more than a flat, concrete floor and white painted walls. There was a staircase at one end.

"Wow, what an incredible space. What was it?" she asked.

"A milking parlour, when we had a dairy herd, but we're just arable now. We decided animals were no longer sustainable after the foot and mouth scares, so we went for diversification in a big way. We still have a small collection of animals, more or less as pets and for visitors, really. They want proper farm holidays so we keep a few animals to pet. I'm little more than a gentleman farmer these days!" He grinned.

"Adam told me a little about it," she said.

"Can I see upstairs? What's there?"

They trooped up the wooden stairs and he unlocked another door at the top.

"It's a fully self-contained flat, though it's too small for a holiday let. I was thinking the whole building could be some sort of studio or light industrial unit. That's why there's nothing there downstairs yet. I'll put in lighting and power and work benches, whatever you need. Anyway, I'll let you explore up here by yourself." He turned to Adam. "Come and have a drink with Martha. She'd love to see you. Come and join us when you're finished, Sophie."

The two men went downstairs and she wandered around this oh-so-perfect modern flat. It really was lovely, with a bit of character left in the original beams. She could hardly believe the rental that Adam had quoted could possibly be correct.

She closed the door and went downstairs and stood in the room below. The work benches would be along the side for sewing, designing and storing work in progress. There was plenty of natural light along this side. Her rails, and a large number more, would be on the opposite side. Even proper wardrobes at some stage. She could have mirrors along the other wall and a large table for cutting in the middle, and there would still be masses of space.

She could hardly wait to move in.

She closed the door behind her and went across to the farm house. She knocked and was welcomed in by a pretty woman a little older than her. "I'm Martha. Do come in, they're in the lounge. What did you think of our conversion?"

"It's just perfect. Everything I could want."

"I wanted the floor to be properly covered in something. I suggested a wooden floor over the concrete. It's expensive but once done, it will last forever," Martha suggested.

"That sounds even better. Concrete tends to be dusty, however well finished it seems."

"Excellent. I'll get Miles to organise it, then."

They went into a lovely, comfortable lounge and the two men rose as they came in.

"What can I get you to drink? And more importantly, do you think the barn will be suitable?"

"White wine, please," Sophie replied, seeing that was what everyone else was drinking. "And yes, it's absolutely perfect for me. But it does depend on the rent . . . I think Adam told you I'm only just starting out. The price Adam told me is very generous of you. I'm sure you could get a lot more."

"Not at all," Miles said. "I'm delighted not to have to go through the dreadful process of getting references and interviewing people and then having to turn them down if we don't like them."

"The floors need finishing, though," Martha told him. "Can you get Stan to do it at the end of the week?"

"Of course. And, Sophie, you must give me a list of exactly what else you need."

It was all too good to be true, Sophie thought. They spent what was left of the evening planning and making proper measurements. Martha and Miles were most enthusiastic and Sophie knew she was going to love working here so close to such nice people.

"Now you must let us know if there's anything else you think of. Stan will make a start on the flooring by Thursday and then he can do benches next week and I'll get my electrician to put in extra sockets and lighting at the same time. I'll block off the corner for a toilet and dressing room — you'll need that if clients call. Shall we say you'll move in maybe two weeks?"

"Yes please!" Sophie smiled. "Goodness,

can you really get everything done in that time?"

"Easily. The men have been working for me for months and I know what they can do. I'll get a rental agreement drawn up and sent to you. Come over any time you want to see it again."

"Thank you so much. I know I'm going to love it here. I'm afraid I shall wake up having dreamed it all."

She couldn't stop talking all the way back to the cottage, making verbal lists of everything she needed to do until she realised Adam was smiling.

"Sorry . . ." she said. "I'm just so excited. It's simply perfect and I can't thank you enough. However did you find it?"

"I think I mentioned before that I play squash with Miles regularly. We met last night and were chatting afterwards. He had told me about his conversion projects before but I'd no idea he had that place among them. I asked him to let me know if he heard of anything and he came up with this suggestion. Do you think you'll be able to pack up in the time — as well as continue your work?"

"Most of the furniture in the cottage belongs there, so it's only a matter of collecting a load of boxes to pack the contents.

There's plenty of built-in wardrobes and things in the new flat and I can always pick up some chests of drawers and other things. I doubt there'll be much time for sitting down in the next few weeks, but once the show is over, I can furnish properly."

"I'm sure Miles will help you out with whatever furnishings you need — he's furnished the holiday lets, after all. I'll come over and help, of course . . . if you'd like, that is? I can borrow one of the company vans to transport everything."

"Thank you so much, Adam. I think I'll be eternally grateful that you invited me to your cousin's wedding. Who could believe anything could be so totally life-changing?"

"I'm glad to help, Sophie, you know I am. Now, make sure you get some sleep." He leaned over and kissed her cheek. "Are you sure you're all right on your own? I could stay over . . . ?"

"I'll be fine — and thank you again."

She almost danced around her room — she couldn't believe how everything was coming together; not just the wedding and the show, but even the prospect of a perfect set-up to live and work — more than she ever could have hoped. Every box ticked, as they said on the property programmes!

She was almost tempted to start packing right away — there were things to get rid of, things to keep. Her workroom was going to be the most difficult to deal with . . . Lists. She needed lists! First thing tomorrow, she must give notice to her landlord.

There was no chance of sleeping for some time so she set to, making her beloved lists, and it was well past midnight before she went to bed.

"I gather you're still excited," Adam said when he phoned the next morning. "We'll have a celebratory dinner on me this evening and I won't take no for an answer."

"Great, thank you! My mind is still buzzing. Oh, Adam, I'm just . . . oh, thank you!"

"I'm glad you're happy," he said rather wistfully. "Perhaps once this is all done and you're settled, we can talk about us?"

Over dinner they planned the move, discussed the venue for the fashion show and arranged the timing for taking photographs for the website.

"I suppose you can forget providing me with a dog to guard me now I'm going to be living in a civilised place," she said, as Adam was driving to the cottage.

"That depends on whether you lock the doors or not."

"They're self-locking there, or didn't you

notice?"

"I bet you lock yourself out more than once!"

"I'll have to keep a key somewhere," she mused. "Anyway, there will always be people around, won't there?"

"You're hopeless, woman!" Adam laughed, but added more seriously, "I won't come in . . . it's too frustrating."

"Whatever do you mean by that?"

He frowned. "As long as you keep putting up barriers, I really don't feel I can be alone with you inside your cottage."

"You make me sound like some sort of ice maiden."

"You behave like it sometimes. Why can't you trust me?"

"It isn't that, Adam. I just don't want to start something I can't finish, especially when I'm launching the business. I need time with you to make sure we have a good future, if we're to have one at all."

"All right, then. Off you go then before I lose heart completely. I'll see you tomorrow."

"I'm still worried about what it might cost. I'm going to be spending a huge chunk of my savings just on the clothes. That's before we start on advertising and all the rest."

"I can use my contacts; I told you, I can do glitz on a budget, so stop worrying. And if I do spend more than you think you can afford, you can pay me back when the show brings you heaps of orders."

Over the next weeks, Sophie felt as if she had worked harder than she had ever worked in her life.

The move to Louden Farm was finally completed and the studio was beginning to seem like her very own. Miles and Martha had done a great job in fitting it out and had also provided several pieces of furniture to make her flat more comfortable and homely.

She sewed from dawn until dusk and gradually, her range was growing. The fifties and sixties sections of the show were almost complete. Her charity shop acquisitions had been given stylish makeovers, using the basic shapes with added trimmings and some chunky jewellery she had collected.

Adam remained in the background for much of the time, leaving her to work. They visited one or two hotels and decided on the venue; it was to take place outside Truro in a hotel where ample parking was available. Adam's contacts included lighting experts and he even had a friend with a music system. Somehow, it seemed he had persuaded them to give their services for free in support of their chosen charity.

"I can't believe you've done so many favours for all these people that they're giving their services for nothing."

"Oh, you'd be surprised. Once you know people it becomes easy to share favours as well as skills," was his enigmatic response. "Besides, it pleases me to be able to help. You are my priority, Sophie."

Sophie felt more and more nervous as the date approached. Though she had been given some experience during her course, the thought of training amateur models how to walk along a catwalk to show off her clothes was daunting. It had to be as professional as possible.

There was also the problem of Rachel. The wedding outfits from Chloe's wedding were going to be a set piece in the show and it had been suggested that the original bridesmaids would all take part. She had also made a group of children's outfits for the beachwear section, which they could model. The children were all excited and promised to behave beautifully — but Rachel looked as if she was going to prove impossible.

"Evidently, she's expecting to be the star

of the whole show," Adam sighed. "She feels she should model any or most of your major items and wants to come and inspect the collection to make her choices!

"I didn't commit to anything but we need to decide how we'll deal with her. She's actually got quite a good shape for a model and is reasonable-looking but I'm just not sure how we can handle the situation."

"As long as she doesn't become some sort of prima donna, I suppose she might be worth considering," Sophie agreed with a shrug. "Besides, I doubt she'll like any of the clothes, but I'll give her a trial anyway. Goodness, it's all really happening isn't it?" Sophie could hardly believe it.

"It certainly is. Now, I need to sit down with you to get the final decisions on photographs for the life-sized posters."

Whatever else she thought about Adam, Sophie had to admit that he was a first class manager. Whoever would have believed that the IT expert she had met during her job as a temp in his office would turn out to be such a dynamic go-getter?

Sophie had to admit, she could never have achieved so much without his backing. He thought of things that had never entered her head.

■ ■ ■ ■

The next afternoon she was busy working when the door was flung open and Rachel came in.

"Hello. So this is your new abode?" she said, surveying Sophie's new work studio. "I must say, it's a bit better than the last one, almost professional. Now, what have you got for me to look at? Adam tells you need me to help out at your little show."

"No, Rachel, Adam told me you wanted to be a part of it. You can model your own bridesmaid's dress and I'll see how you look in one or two of the other things."

"Well, if I have to come anyway, I might as well see if there's anything else."

Sophie gave a sigh and put down the piece she was working on. For the next half hour, Rachel picked along her rails of finished clothes and shook her head on numerous occasions.

"I suppose some of these aren't too bad but most of them are quite out of the question. Are you sure it's wise for them to be seen by the public? Some of them are much too short or too . . . well, plain odd. Who on earth do you expect to buy them?"

"Young folk like to be different, Rachel.

I'm trying to cater for a whole range of people. You can try on one or two of the things if you like. There's a screen in the corner you can use."

"No proper fitting rooms, then?"

"Not yet . . . soon." Sophie controlled her temper and smiled.

Rachel emerged from behind the screen wearing one of Sophie's more conventional dress and jacket outfits in a sage green that complemented her red hair and slim figure. She hated to admit it, but the woman looked good and showed off the outfit to its best advantage.

"That looks great on you," she said.

"Not all that bad, actually," Rachel conceded. "Fine, I'll model this one. There's an evening dress I quite like too. I'll try that one next."

Sophie decided to give her free rein to select things and continued with the sewing she had been doing, watching carefully to see the effect of the clothes.

"I must say," Rachel admitted, "one or two of these things are a surprise to me. I'm beginning to see why Adam thinks he can help you out. He's quite the New Age Man, being involved with your fashion show. I wasn't enthusiastic at all when dear Adam suggested it would help you out of a hole, but I can spare a little of my time. Besides, it gives Adam and me a chance to be together for a while."

"How very generous of you," Sophie said, tongue in cheek. "There's a rehearsal here the weekend after next, on the Sunday. Then there'll be a dress rehearsal at the hotel the day before the show. I have a hairdresser and make-up artist coming over during the rehearsal."

"Sundays aren't good for me," Rachel announced haughtily.

"It has to be a Sunday because of everyone's work commitments. If you can't manage it, then I'll have to turn down your kind offer," Sophie said firmly.

"Very well, if you insist, I expect I can arrange something."

"Fine. I'll label the clothes you like and set them to one side."

"Actually, you said the wedding outfits were to be the finale, I believe? I think I should wear the bridal gown. Chloe and I are about the same size and it would be a pity to allow someone to wear it who wouldn't show it at its best."

"But you'll be wearing your own bridesmaid outfit, Rachel."

"Surely, the bridal gown is the most important item?"

"I'll give it some thought. It depends on the rest of the girls who are coming to model."

Rachel looked sulky at not getting her own way. She desperately wanted to wear the beautiful bridal gown for reasons of her own — if Adam saw her looking so beautiful, who could tell what ideas he might have?

"I want to make sure the clothes are modelled by the best people for the look I want to achieve," Sophie went on, unaware of Rachel's thoughts. "Now, if there's nothing else, I won't keep you any longer. Thanks for coming and I'm pleased you like some of my designs."

"Like may be a bit of an exaggeration. You'd better give me your new phone number in case I have any queries."

"It's the same, I had it transferred."

"That went better than I thought," Sophie murmured to herself after Rachel had left. Strangely, the tempered compliments made her feel better. She smiled at the thought of Rachel wanting to wear the bridal gown and wondered at her motivation. Perhaps she just liked being centre stage. Still, she had to admit that Rachel had looked particularly good in some of the clothes. Her striking colouring made many of the outfits quite unsuitable for her so it was good to know there were some at least that pleased her.

Adam remained constantly amazed at the amount of things she had produced single-handed.

"You're quite astounding. I thought you'd need to bring in a seamstress to help, but somehow you've managed."

"Only because you've done virtually everything else. I could never have managed to think of so many things and bring it all together the way you've done."

"I think we make a good team," he said with a smile.

"I'm hoping this is just the start of a whole new future."

"I hope so too," he said somewhat wistfully. "Oh, by the way, I've drafted a press release for the local papers. Will you cast your eye over it? I need to send it next week . . . perhaps to the local radio too; they have a 'what's on' thing and any publicity will be good. Ticket sales might need a boost — I've sent out quite a few as freebies, some contacts from up-country . . . oh, and Marnie's still planning to come over from the States. Mum's delighted — she hasn't seen her for ages."

"You hardly stop for breath, do you?" Sophie laughed. "You are truly amazing, Adam Gilbert."

"The feeling's mutual. Come here, I haven't had so much as a hug in days." He pulled her to him and they both felt the surge of emotion that they had been trying to stifle for so long. As he bent to kiss her, he felt her body soften towards him and his heart raced. "My darling Sophie," he murmured.

She stiffened momentarily and he drew away. "It's all right. I know what a demanding time this is for you. I can wait a little longer."

"Oh, Adam, I'm sorry. It won't be long now, I promise. It's just that I daren't stop. I need at least six more things to add to some of the groups. And I need to make an expedition round some charity shops for some pieces of jewellery . . ."

"Why don't I ask some of the major stores to loan us some pieces for the show? I'm sure they'll oblige for a little publicity."

"I'd never dare ask!"

"Tell me what you want and I'll see what I can do. We haven't finally printed the programme yet so I can easily put in some extra acknowledgements."

She made her list, smiling at the thought of this handsome man chatting up the managers of various stores. She had to admit to feeling a slight pang of jealousy.

Now why should she feel like that? He had made it very clear that he wanted her.

Her happy smile faded as the phone rang and she left the answering machine to pick it up.

"Why don't you pick up? I know you're there," said a deep, cracked voice. "You've had your own way too long. Watch out." There was a pause and a long blast of the same whistle she had heard before.

"Damn you," she whispered. Someone was trying to spoil everything again.

CHAPTER 12

The weekend of the rehearsal arrived. Several of the potential models had visited the workshop during the previous week and Sophie had sorted out who was going to wear which clothes. Large name labels had been attached to the hangers with plastic bags containing accessories.

It had been decided that everyone should provide their own shoes to ensure safe passage along the catwalk; wearing unfamiliar shoes could have been a disaster and most of the girls had some special shoes that were suitable.

Rachel had arrived with the rest and was beginning to irritate both Sophie and some of the others, styling herself as star of the entire show. Adam had to step in and save the situation from turning ugly.

"Maybe you'd like to come for a drink and a bite to eat," he offered. "There's a pub nearby."

"That would be great," Rachel agreed enthusiastically.

Sophie cast him a grateful look. She had organised plates of sandwiches for everyone and without Rachel, the whole place would have a much more relaxed atmosphere.

She could even forgive her enemy's smug look as she went off arm-in-arm with him, her head leaning close to his. She had got her own way with the wedding dress, and two of the other girls were going to wear the adult bridesmaids' outfits.

Towards the end of the afternoon, Sophie called for quiet.

"Thank you all so much. I'm sure the event is all going to go very smoothly. I've made a note of all the alterations and additions that are needed and I'll make sure they're all done by Wednesday night. Can I see you all at the Porthwest Hotel by six-thirty on Wednesday evening, please? We're in the Mulberry Suite — just ask at reception if you don't know it. See you then, and again, thank you."

There were murmurs of pleasure from the assembled girls and several said how much they had enjoyed themselves.

After they'd all left, Sophie slumped down on her chair. She felt exhausted, but happy with the way things were going. She glanced at her watch. It was four-thirty and Adam had not returned with Rachel after their lunch.

She felt absurdly jealous. Where could they have gone? A pub lunch surely couldn't go on for this length of time. Perhaps he'd taken her home? But her car was still here.

The woman was always keen to be with Adam and had once had high hopes they might become engaged. They were only very distantly related so there were no actual taboos on them having a relationship — except that Adam had always said he was not interested.

There was nothing she could do except wait for their return. She put the kettle on for tea and sat with her many lists. A few items needed altering and some needed additional trimmings or hems taking up, nothing too drastic.

She heard a car stop and looked out. It was Adam and a very happy-looking Rachel.

"We've had a wonderful afternoon," she

said with a big grin on her face. "Adam took me for a gorgeous walk. I haven't been out in the fresh air for far too long. Clearly, I needed the inspiration of this handsome man."

"That was nice," Sophie said, almost through gritted teeth. "We all enjoyed ourselves, too. The girls have just gone home and I'm going through my list of alterations I need to do before Wednesday. I've just made some tea, if you'd like some."

"Great," Adam said. "How about you, Rachel?"

"Have you any Earl Grey?"

"No," Sophie snapped. "No pretensions here."

"Then, I think not, thanks all the same."

"We won't keep you, then. Adam and I have a whole heap of things to talk through before the rehearsal."

"I'll stick around. Adam and I are going on somewhere for the evening." Rachel couldn't keep a smirk from her face.

Sophie glanced at Adam who gave a shrug.

"In that case, perhaps you'd prefer to meet tomorrow evening?" she suggested to him.

"If you like. I expect you're probably feeling tired now anyway." Adam seemed calm and did not indicate he objected to Rachel's suggestion, as he usually did. To Sophie, it seemed almost as if he'd had a complete change of heart.

Sophie felt her own heart give a twist but she tried to sound matter-of-fact. "Fine. I have plenty to do. If you can spare the time tomorrow, we can discuss everything then."

"I'll come, too," Rachel chimed in happily. "I'm sure there are plenty of suggestions I can make to ensure things look much more professional."

Sophie felt her temper rising and bit her lip to stop herself from saying something she might regret. She hoped Adam would make a comment but he remained silent as he sipped his tea. What was going on? Had she played the ice queen once too often? Had Rachel finally got her way and enticed Adam away from her? Of all the times for this to happen! She was about to have her own fashion show and properly launch her label, and all of it thanks to Adam. Surely he wouldn't let her down at this crucial point in her life?

"I'm sure we'll manage, thank you, Rachel," she managed to mumble. "What do you think, Adam?"

"I'm easy," he shrugged. "If Rachel wants to be a part of it, I've no objections."

Sophie could hardly believe her ears. This was the Adam who professed to care so deeply about her and who had always said he felt nothing for the wretched Rachel!

"That's that then," Rachel purred. "All right if I leave my car here? I might as well — then Adam can drop me back at my place tonight and collect me tomorrow."

"No problem," Sophie said, tight-lipped. She had been intending to offer to cook for Adam the next evening, but no way was she about to include Rachel in her offer. "I'll see you both tomorrow evening. Now if you'll excuse me, I need to start work on my alterations."

As soon as they were gone, she almost ran up the stairs, tears threatening to overwhelm her. If Adam really felt anything for her, he would never have allowed this situation to get so out of hand. But there was no one to blame but herself.

Too late, she realised Adam was the man she loved; she loved him body and soul and knew she should have admitted it a long time ago.

All the times he had sworn to her that he had no feelings for Rachel and yet now he was willingly spending time with her, taking her out — and who could tell where he intended sleeping that evening? Rachel had manipulated everything so that he was taking her home and collecting her the following day.

It must have been after seeing Rachel look so gorgeous in Chloe's wedding dress. She had to admit, it really had looked perfect on her, curse the woman!

Sophie splashed cold water on her face and took deep breaths before going back down to the workroom, put on some loud music and began to work.

She continued to work until well after ten o'clock and she was almost dropping with fatigue. She had eaten nothing since a sandwich at lunchtime and felt quite faint. She knew she ought to eat something but anything she could think of made her feel positively sick.

She made her usual hot chocolate and sat nursing the mug in her icy hands, but even that wasn't as comforting as usual so she went to bed and fell into a deep sleep of exhaustion.

When she woke at four o'clock, for a moment she couldn't think why she felt so down, but then it all came flooding back and she knew that sleep was over for the night. She might as well go downstairs and do some more work.

She made some toast and coffee and felt slightly better, telling herself she was so lucky not to have to face the Monday morning grind into work and, having given herself a good dose of positive thinking, she set to work. With the extra time she had gained last night and her early start today, she could easily put together the outfits she felt were lacking.

It was just past nine when her phone rang. It had to be Adam with an apology, she thought — she hoped.

"Is that the Sophie of Design by Sophie?"

"It is. Who's calling?"

"Western Television here, Jemima Gray. I have your press release about your forthcoming show. Adam Gilbert's behind it, I understand?"

"Well, he's assisting me in putting it together, yes."

"I assumed so. We'd like to come and do an interview with you, have a look at your set-up. We'd hope to put it out on our evening news bulletin. Are you free this morning?"

"Oh . . . well, yes . . . I suppose so . . ." She was stammering like a baby but this was a chance in a million. How had Adam managed this one? "Yes," she said after a deep, calming breath. "I'd be delighted if you could come over."

"Great. It'll just be a short interview,

maybe look at some of the outfits for the show and you can tell us your background and how you got started. Eleven o'clock okay?"

"Perfect," she replied having recovered herself. She rushed around tidying and changed into a simple, close-fitting dress in navy. She added some costume jewellery and a floaty scarf, then she phoned Adam.

"Hi. Do you know a Jemima Gray?"

"Jem? Yes, she was at uni with me. Why?"

"She just called. She's coming over to do an interview, for Western Television! Did you organise it?"

"I sent them a press release. Are you all right with it?"

"I guess so. It was a bit of a shock but I'm ready for her now. What a great bit of advertising — thanks."

"All part of the service," he said. "Are you okay?"

"Of course. Why wouldn't I be?" she said sharply.

"You seemed a bit down last night."

Suddenly all Sophie's pent-up anger and frustration came pouring out and she just couldn't help herself. "Can you blame me after seeing you all cosy with Rachel? Anyway, it's no problem — I hope it all works out for you." She bit her lip. "I must go, they'll be here soon."

"Sophie, wait! Listen — I . . ."

In her anger she hung up. She didn't want to hear excuses.

This interview may be the biggest chance she ever had for mass publicity and she needed to concentrate.

Sophie briefly wondered if she should phone her parents and tell them to watch later? She decided to leave it until after the recording and then she would have a better idea of when it might be screened.

She heard the car stop and went out to greet Jemima and her colleague.

"Hi, Sophie. Good of you to see us on such short notice. This is Geoff, my cameraman."

"Hello. Thank you for coming."

"So, how's the lovely Adam? Are you two together?"

"Just business," she replied firmly. If she'd been asked that at any other time, she would have blushed and admitted that they were more than business partners.

"He's a great guy. We had a bit of a thing going at uni but then went our different ways. So is he married yet?"

"No, I'm not sure what's going on in his life at present. Please come in. Can I get you some coffee?"

"That would be good. Geoff can wander round while we talk a little, then we'll start the interview. You can tell me how it started and your plans for the future."

They chatted casually for about half an hour until Sophie felt relaxed, while Jemima had made some notes and decided what she wanted to ask.

"If you're ready, we'll start some takes . . . perhaps you'd like to sit by your sewing machine. If you need to stop, or if you feel you've gone wrong, it's no problem, we can edit it out later. Then we can take shots of some of the clothes and use your speech over them . . . that all sound okay?"

They recorded for almost half an hour and by the end, Sophie was surprised to feel quite exhausted.

"It will only be a short feature, probably five minutes max, but we always like to have plenty of film to ~~must~~ make sure we have what we need."

Jemima was charming and very pretty, Sophie thought. "When's it likely to be shown?" she asked.

"Well, unless anything major breaks between now and this evening, after the six o'clock news bulletin. I must say, I love your designs, especially the period stuff. Is any of it for sale?"

"It all will be after the show, but for the moment, I need everything here."

"And have you made the whole lot yourself, no help?"

"Yes, I did actually. I don't have any staff at this stage, but if the label takes off, then I will have to start looking for workers."

"I might try to get to the show. I admire your enterprise."

Once they had left, Sophie rushed to call her mother, who was out but she left a message telling her parents to watch the news that evening. Then she went to tell Martha and Miles and ended up staying for lunch with them.

"I really should be working but I appreciate the break," she told them.

"It's not every day we get to entertain a television star in our own kitchen," Martha said with a smile. "Where's Adam today? We haven't seen him much lately."

"I expect he's at work. He's taking a couple of days off later in the week for the show, so he has to make sure everything is running smoothly at the office. He's coming over this evening to discuss the final plans."

"Why don't you both come over for a

drink when you've finished?" Martha offered.

"Thanks but . . . well . . . he's bringing Rachel with him."

"But I thought you and he . . . Sorry, I must have misunderstood. Bring Rachel, too, of course."

"I think we might be a bit late finishing." Sophie scrambled around for an excuse. "Another time, perhaps?"

It was all just too much. Sharing Adam with someone else was unfamiliar to her and she hated trying to sound as if it didn't matter. It hurt so much but she had no one to blame but herself.

As it was, they arrived soon after seven. Rachel had her arm firmly linked through Adam's, very possessively, proving they were together. Sophie had cleared a space on the work table and set some chairs beside it. She had sheets of paper and pens ready and her own lists of things to discuss.

"How did the interview go?" Adam asked her.

"Didn't you see it? I thought it was fine. My parents were thrilled — they called me after they'd seen it."

"Did you record it?" Adam asked. "Can we go up and see it? I expect Jemima is as pretty as ever, she's a lovely woman."

"I'm afraid we missed it — we were having supper then, weren't we, darling?" Rachel said, making sure Sophie knew they'd been together. "Don't you think we should be getting on with whatever Sophie wants to say? I don't want to be too late again. It was very late last night, wasn't it, before either of us got any sleep?"

She smirked at Adam who looked most uncomfortable.

Sophie looked away when she stroked his hand; it was just too much. She couldn't decide if she wanted to throw up or chuck a bucket of water over the pair of them.

How could he?

"Perhaps we'd better get on with the business. If there's time later, I can play the recording to you," she said.

"As you like," Adam replied, unusually unenthusiastic.

They settled down to talk through the finer details of what needed doing and when. Adam's music friend had been briefed about the various tracks they would need and the lighting expert was setting up on Wednesday evening. Fortunately, the conference centre wasn't being used so they could set everything up before the dress rehearsal. Adam was going to do the commentary.

"Is it all right if I write the basic script by Wednesday?" Sophie asked. "Only there may be one or two extra items included, if I can finish them in time. I leave it to you to add your own comments and a few light-hearted things."

"That's fine, though I admit, I'm a bit nervous about it."

"You'll be wonderful, darling," Rachel purred, moving closer to him. He seemed to have no objection and Sophie couldn't believe that he was anything but happy with his new lady friend.

"The tickets have gone well," he said blandly. "We should get more inquiries now people have seen the television interview. The charity shop in town has sold quite a few and they're coming to set up their stall on Thursday afternoon."

"Good. If there's nothing else?" Sophie asked. "I won't keep you any longer, I'm sure you have things to do." Sophie surprised herself at the ring of jealousy in her tone. "I'll make a copy of my interview and you can watch it some other time. I was up early today and I'm tired."

"As you like," Adam said again. "Call me tomorrow if you think of anything else, otherwise I'll be here bright and early on Wednesday with the van."

"I'll be here, too," Rachel added. "We can't have you struggling on your own."

Sophie couldn't even bring herself to speak.

"Shall I drive off first or follow you?" Rachel asked Adam.

At least she was removing her car from in front of her flat, Sophie was pleased to note.

Adam hesitated as he was going out and looked at Sophie as if he was going to say something, but he gave her a thin smile instead and left.

Sophie shut the door firmly and leaned back on it, suddenly exhausted. Of all the times for things to have reached this point!

Still, she was confident she would still have his full support for this endeavour, despite the fact she would also have to put up with Rachel hovering around most of the time.

Once this show was over, she could thank them both for their help and then they could go off into the sunset or wherever they wanted to go. There would be no reason for her ever to run into Adam again.

It was hard to believe the man she had believed to be so thoughtful and kind and too good to be true really was too good to be true! She was just so relieved that she hadn't followed her heart all those weeks ago. How could he flaunt Rachel in front of her like this? She would never have put him down as downright cruel. At least she had plenty of work to do to see her through the next two days.

Early the following morning, two local newspaper journalists came to see Sophie. Evidently, seeing her piece on the news the previous evening had sparked interest and she was kept busy with interviews and photographers for much of the morning. The papers all came out on Thursday, in good time for the show. There were still a few tickets left and this would surely be good for a sellout.

It looked as if it was going to be a success, assuming people actually bought or ordered some of the clothes. If they didn't, she was in trouble. Most of her savings had gone and though Chloe's wedding payments had covered her rent for several weeks, she had little to fall back on. It was all adding to her stress but all the same she was bubbling with excitement inside.

Adam and Rachel? Who needed them!

As if reading her mind, Adam phoned. "How's things?" he asked, sounding more like the Adam she thought she'd known.

"Fine. I've just done interviews with the

local papers."

"That's terrific. I've got the large poster photographs here. They've just been sent up from the printers and they look amazing. Would you like me to bring them over for you to see before tomorrow?"

"That's good of you but I still have heaps to do and I'm sure you have better things to do with your evening. Thanks anyway, must get on — bye." Sophie simply could not bear the thought of another evening with Rachel draping herself all over him. Tomorrow would be bad enough.

She spent the rest of the day ironing and making sure everything was ready to go. They had worked out that the clothes would be loaded into the van on the rails, so they would not be crumpled in transit. The logistics were complicated and it would already mean two trips for Adam. Dare she ring him and see if he had any suggestions?

"Adam? Sorry to bother you," she said, trying to sound brisk. "But do you know anyone who might have another dress rail? I thought one of the shops near the office might lend us one?"

"Leave it with me. I have a minor crisis in the office at the moment, but I'll see what I can do."

She'd heard no more from him that day

and decided that she should check through everything just once more. She had every reason to be proud of her efforts and at least she had put everything she could into this, her one big chance.

Her mother was coming down for the show and would be staying in the flat with her afterwards. At least that might help cushion the blow when she and Adam finally parted company. He would have to return everything to the workshop on Friday. Hopefully, once that was done she could get on with the rest of her life.

Sophie was down in her workroom early the next day. Too excited to sleep and with far too many things racing round her tired brain, she checked and re-checked, hoping she had thought of everything. Finally, it was all coming together and once the dress rehearsal was over, she could relax a little.

Determined to stay calm throughout the day and evening, she put her many lists into her handbag — nothing could be forgotten. She made coffee as she waited for Adam's arrival. The large van drove into the yard and stopped outside, with Rachel's snazzy sports car stopped close behind.

"Morning, Sophie. It looks as if you're all organised."

"I hope so. I've made coffee if you'd like some," she offered.

"We had breakfast just before we came out," Rachel replied pointedly. "So not for me, thanks."

"I'd love one, thanks." Adam glared at Rachel and was about to say something, but Sophie interrupted.

"Did you have any luck with the extra rail?"

"It's in the van. I borrowed it from that little shop along from the office. They're doing a refurb and having built-in fixtures so it's yours for keeps if you want it."

"Fantastic," Sophie replied. "We're ready to start loading once you've finished your coffee."

"It looks as if you've got even more things," Rachel remarked as she pushed things along the rails.

"Be careful you don't crease anything, please," Sophie said. "Actually, I'd better put in an iron and ironing board."

When they arrived at the hotel, the large function room had a stage at one end and numerous curtains to screen off areas. Hotel staff were at their disposal to help organise and were soon busy arranging the stage as a catwalk and bringing in chairs to surround it.

It all looked perfect and Sophie was delighted.

"What do you think of these?" Adam said proudly unpacking the giant photographs he'd had printed. They had stands fixed to the back and would line the entrance, and there was a large banner to be hung at the back of the stage with her logo printed in massive letters.

"Oh wow, they're fantastic! Oh, Adam, I can't believe it's all really happening." She felt quite tearful at the sight of all these very professional-looking additions to the room.

"Excuse me, where do you want the drinks table?" one of the hotel staff asked. Adam quickly turned away from her and spoke to him as they walked away. She assumed he must have been referring to the charity's table and continued to organise everything in the dressing room.

The dress rehearsal went perfectly. The various groups of clothes worked well together and everyone had plenty of time to change, provided nobody panicked. If they had all been professional models, Sophie couldn't have wished for more. She needed to press one or two things before the show itself but apart from that, she had little more to do. Even the jewellery Adam had borrowed from yet another of his contacts had worked well, adding extra glamour.

By ten o'clock, everyone except Sophie, Adam — and inevitably Rachel — had left.

"Stop tidying up," Adam told Sophie gently. "Everything is perfect and you need to get some rest so you're ready for your big day. I'd never have believed one person could have done so much in the time. You really are quite amazing."

"Thank you so much for all your help and encouragement. I could never have done it without you behind me . . ."

"You certainly fell on your feet when you picked him up," Rachel interrupted.

"I suppose I did," Sophie replied, forcing a smile. She was not going to bite whatever Rachel said to try to bait her.

"How on earth you thought you could put together something like this without proper financial support, I'll never know," Rachel continued to goad. "It was really quite naïve of you."

"Rachel . . ." Adam said, a warning in his tone.

"Oh, sorry. You mean she doesn't know you've been bankrolling her all this time?"

"Whatever do you mean?" Sophie was genuinely puzzled.

"You can't seriously think you could rent your wonderful workroom and flat for what you're paying? But good old Miles is such a walkover that he went along with it," Rachel told her with obvious glee. "And renting this suite here — they're not a charity, you know. The wine and canapés alone will cost more than you could earn in a month."

"Rachel, that's enough!" Adam hissed, his voice low and dangerous. "You should be going now."

"Not without you, Adam," Rachel went on. "I'm not leaving you here with that money-grasping . . . she'll worm her way into your life again and try to con you into something you'll regret for ever more. I've tried everything I can to put her off — I even tried frightening her out of her cottage, kept her awake with phone calls, but still she clings on to you. Can't you see what she's doing?" she ranted on, completely unable to see what she herself was doing. "She's just a pathetic little gold-digger!"

"So it was you!" Sophie gasped. "The calls, the break-in . . . it wouldn't surprise me if you'd even organised the biker gang!" Sophie was overcome with rage. "And I can pay my own way," she hissed. "If Adam has made payments I know nothing about, I shall of course repay him in full. I had no idea and believed everything he told me about doing deals with contacts. And as for my rent, if indeed it is much more, then I shall have to rethink the whole thing."

Her heart was hammering and she couldn't believe what was happening. "Now I think it really is time you left. Together."

As the pair left the room, Sophie could hear their angry, raised voices from the main hall but she did not want to hear what was being said. She felt as if everything was about to come crashing down around her.

Why had Rachel picked this of all times to make her announcements — and more to the point, why hadn't Adam denied the accusations? It could only mean one thing: they were true. So be it. She would pay for it, one way or another.

He was just as bad as Sam — just another control freak and she was extremely lucky she had never given in to him.

CHAPTER 13

When she thought the coast was clear, Sophie switched the lights off and went through to the main hall. There was a bad taste in her mouth as she looked at the banner, the giant pictures of her clothes and all the things that had delighted her so much. Now it seemed she was no more than an amateur who believed she had accomplished so much by her own endeavours. How could she have been so stupid?

"Sophie?"

She spun round at the sound of Adam's quiet voice. "Oh! I thought you'd both left."

"Rachel's gone. I'm so sorry she had that outburst . . ."

"Well, at least I know the truth now. You two must have had plenty of laughs at my expense, chatting over your cosy meals together. I can't believe I was so naïve — again! Well, I meant what I said; somehow, I'll pay you back." She turned away from him again, flushing with shame. "How much extra is the rent? I questioned you at the time. Even Miles must have been in on the deal. I'll never dare look them in the face again."

"Please, listen to me," Adam pleaded. "Rachel was making it up about the rent — and other things besides. Miles is perfectly happy with what you are paying. He's also seriously impressed with what you're doing."

"What about all of this?" She swept her arm round the room.

"We have to make it as good as we can. It's normal to provide such refreshments at a glitzy do like this."

"But you did it all without consulting me."

"You'd have said no, wouldn't you?"

"Probably the thing that hurts is you and Rachel being together," Sophie raged, aware only of her own pain. "After everything you said about her. You said you couldn't stand her and here you are spending days — and nights — together."

"We've not spent a single night together. She exaggerates."

"Oh, come on! Breakfasts? Not sleeping much? Let's stop right there! I don't want to hear any more lies. I am truly grateful to you for everything but once tomorrow's over, let's call it a day. I'll send you a cheque for what I owe when the show's over and I have some cash coming in."

"Sophie, please. You must listen to me. Rachel and I —"

"No! I don't have to listen to your lies any more! I'll speak to Miles and make sure the bit about the rent is at least true. I'll see you tomorrow. Goodnight."

She swept out of the room and didn't look back.

Sophie had a long soak in the bath and drank a glass of wine as she lay there, her scented candles supposedly inducing some sort of relaxation. Nothing was working. She feared a sleepless night ahead and cursed herself for letting herself become so stressed. She should be on top of the world and well-rested before the biggest event in her entire life. Instead, she was worried about being made to look a fool by a silly woman who had been jealous of her.

So what if Rachel had won Adam? She had her own ambitions and Rachel could keep him, if that's what they both wanted. Yes, she loved him . . . but fortunately, she was the only person in the world who knew that. She'd get over it, just as she'd got over her previous relationship.

The next morning she had made up a bed in the living room for her mother to sleep on and everything was ready; there was nothing more to be done. She wandered round the workroom tidying already tidy shelves. It looked bare and empty without all her clothes filling the rails.

Someone knocked at the door.

"I don't know if you've seen the papers yet," Martha said. "You're on the front page! Well, at least it's a leader for the article later. There's a lovely picture of you and several of the garments. There's a feature in the other paper too. I'll leave them with you, Miles can pick up extra copies later," she went on excitedly. "Well done, you! I'm so looking forward to this evening. Are you all ready?"

"I think so, though I'm sure there must be heaps I've forgotten," Sophie replied. "But . . . I need to have a talk with you and Miles at some point very soon — tomorrow, perhaps?"

"Oh dear, I hope there's nothing wrong?"

"Just something I need to clear up." She was interrupted by the phone. "Sorry, I need to answer this."

"Miss James? Sophie? It's the Porthwest Hotel here. One of your models came in earlier and asked to be let into the conference suite. I thought I'd better check it was all right."

"One of the models? Do you know who?"

"The redhead. Tall, striking lady."

"Have you let her in?"

"Well, yes . . . she was very insistent. Something about leaving her bag there last night. I assumed it would be all right . . ."

"I'll come over right away. I'll be there in about fifteen minutes. Thanks for the call."

"Is everything all right?" Martha asked.

"I hope so. I have to go to the hotel."

"Would you like me to come with you? You sound worried."

"Actually, if you'd like to come, I'd appreciate it. It's Rachel. I'm sure she's up to

234

something."

"Give me a minute to grab my things and tell Miles."

They drove as fast as her little car allowed. Rachel's car was parked near the entrance when they arrived and the two rushed inside. The main hall stood as it had been left, looking ready for the event. The dressing room door was closed but she could hear movement inside.

They tried to push the door open but something was blocking it. Sophie heaved her shoulder against it until it finally gave way — and there Rachel stood, scissors in hand, about to shred the glorious wedding dress.

"Rachel!" Sophie screamed.

"If I can't have him, then why should you? You think you're so clever, you little gold digger! Well — this is what I think of you and your silly show!"

She plunged the scissors into the silk skirt and ripped down the entire length of it. Sophie was frozen to the spot but Martha rushed towards her, wrestled the scissors from Rachel's grasp and pushed her away. Rachel fell to the ground and lay there panting; she looked positively manic. Sophie looked at the ruined dress and burst into tears. It was to have been the highlight of the whole show and Rachel had ruined it.

But that wasn't all; as Sophie looked at the rails of clothes she'd lovingly made, pressed and ready to be shown off, she saw that Rachel's scissors had done their worst. At least half a dozen of her prize exhibits had suffered.

"Can you do anything to repair them?" Martha asked.

"No point!" Rachel gloated as she clambered to her feet. "I won't be here to model them! Adam is going to come away with me!" She rushed out, leaving the two women utterly confused.

"I think she must have had some sort of breakdown. We should warn Adam. Who knows what she will do next?" Martha said. She took hold of a bereft Sophie and tried to rally her spirits. "Meanwhile, we need to see what can be repaired. Have you got a sewing machine here?"

"I didn't think I'd need it . . ." Sophie said, defeated.

"I'll call Miles. He can get into your workshop and bring yours over. Thank goodness we arrived when we did. Now, tell me what I can do to help and then go and call Adam."

"Have you seen Rachel today?" she asked Adam numbly.

"No. We had a huge row and she stormed off. Why?"

Sophie explained what had happened. "I think she must have had some sort of breakdown," she repeated Martha's words.

"Oh, my God, Sophie! How much damage has she done?"

"Loads. I can probably repair some things with Martha's help, but there's so little time — and I'm a model short. She'd picked out most of the best items for herself. She wanted to be the star of the evening."

"The woman's gone seriously mad. If you can repair enough of the clothes, I may have a solution for the model. Remember my sister Marnie? She arrived last night. I think she's probably the same size as Rachel. She'd be thrilled to take her place."

Somehow, the rows and arguments and terrible feeling of being let down by Adam had all evaporated. This new crisis was far worse.

"This gorgeous wedding dress," Martha sighed, shaking her head at the devastating slit that ruined the line of the front panel. "If I join it together, can you disguise it in some way?"

"I suppose we could get a bouquet with a trail of ribbons or something. I can put in a stitch to make sure it covers the damage.

But there's so little time before the show . . ."

"Why don't I go out and see what I can find?"

"Bless you, Martha. Thank goodness you came with me. Some of the other things will be easier to manage. Why on earth did she have to be so vindictive? She knew how much this meant to me."

"That's your answer. From what I remember of her, she never had much to occupy her. Her father always indulged her in whatever she wanted. I used to know her from boarding school days, she was a real horror. Right. I'll go see what I can find."

"Here, take my car." Sophie handed her keys to Martha.

Mere moments later, Adam arrived. He had been working in the office when she called, still trying to sort out the problems from a couple of days ago. He looked at all the damage and his heart bled for the girl who had worked so hard for this day.

"I can't tell you how sorry I am," he said.

"It's not your fault." Sophie was still distraught.

"But it is. I've been so stupid. I thought if I spent some time with Rachel, I'd keep her out of your hair and it might even be a help to you getting the show ready. Only I got it all terribly wrong and she started making ridiculous assumptions. I was going to put her right as soon as the show was over." Adam looked shell-shocked as he went on. "But when she poured out all those lies last night, I realised I had to deal with it sooner rather than later. She followed me home and insisted she was going to spend the night with me. When I wasn't having it she went absolutely berserk. After a mega scene, I finally pushed her out at about three o'clock and she roared off up the road disturbing half the neighbourhood."

"And so she blamed it all on me and took her revenge," Sophie murmured. "It might have been helpful if you'd told me about this scheme of yours. I've been thinking all sorts of dreadful things about you since Sunday."

"I did try to speak to you on several occasions . . ."

"I didn't want to listen though, did I?" Sophie admitted.

"We'll talk about it later — what can I do to help now?"

"If you can iron, there'll be lots after I've done the repairs."

"I'm quite the expert, as it happens."

Miles arrived with the sewing machine within minutes and Sophie began to work.

With some clever stitching and embroidery, most things were salvageable. She worked solidly through the afternoon and ate the sandwiches that Adam put before her. Martha managed to find a silk bouquet and tied long trails of ribbons to hide the extra seam down what should have been the smooth flat panel at the front.

Sophie was so busy, she barely noticed the tall, dark woman who had come into the changing room. Her bright blue eyes should have told her she was looking at Adam's sister Marnie, but she was far too preoccupied to take in anything.

"I'm Marnie, ready and willing to help in any way I can." The accent had a definite American twang to it, from her years of living in New York. "Chloe told me what a huge talent you have."

"Hello, Marnie, pleased to meet you. I'm sorry, I'm just trying to make sure everything's in order after . . . well, I suppose Adam's told you?"

"Rachel? A deeply disturbed woman." She was looking at a range of cocktail and party dresses. Sophie had used several different colours of antique lace short jackets over shiny fabrics so the jewel colours shone through. "You have some great things here. I love these — they would go down a storm in New York. I'll have to take a couple for myself."

"Thank you, that's a great start. I'd like to make sure the clothes fit you properly . . . Heavens. What time is it?"

"Five o'clock."

"I haven't even got my own outfit here for the evening. And my mum will be arriving any moment. I need to get back to my place and change. Will you be okay if I leave you?"

"Off you go," Adam told her. "I'll see to everything while you're away, but be quick."

As Sophie drove home, she couldn't believe everything that had happened. How could she have got into such a mess?

With only half an hour to dress for the most important evening of her life and her mother was parked outside already.

She rushed her upstairs, telling her tale of woe as she went.

"Sorry, Mum, but I must hurry. I've got to change and get back to the hotel in zero time. Make yourself at home. Bathroom's through there . . ."

"It's lovely, this flat of yours. So much nicer than that isolated cottage. And the workroom. You're a lucky girl."

"Did you want tea? Or can you wait till we get to the hotel?"

"I'll wait, dear. You're obviously rather

flustered. I thought you might be, but after what you've told me about that awful woman, it's not surprising. Dad sends his love and hopes you won't mind that he's not here but it isn't his sort of thing. Besides, he's looking after the animals." She turned just as Sophie came into the room in her outfit. "Wow, you look gorgeous, love. That colour makes your eyes look even greener . . . I never did work out where you inherited them."

"Come on then. There will be nibbles and things at the show. Or I can get someone to make you a sandwich. I was thinking we might eat afterwards. It won't be late finishing."

Like a whirlwind, Sophie's mother was whisked out to the car and they drove back to the hotel.

It was a hive of activity in the dressing room as everyone was arriving and clamouring for attention.

They'd all heard about Rachel's vicious attack and marvelled at the repairs. Sophie introduced her mother, donned an overall and set to work to make sure everything was exactly as she wanted it to be.

Adam and her mother seemed to be ensconced in a corner, chatting nineteen to the dozen but she couldn't care less. It was all way beyond her control.

As the lights dimmed, promptly at seven-thirty, Sophie held her breath. This was it.

The music began and the first of the girls walked along the catwalk. There was spontaneous applause. The music died and Adam made his welcome speech, introduced the girls in turn and named the outfits as they were paraded. He was an absolute natural and had the audience eating out of his hand.

"Our next section is a very special one, close to Sophie's heart," he announced. "She calls this the vintage collection and most of these items have been re-styled from, what's the phrase? Previously enjoyed garments."

The audience applauded. The range was definitely of its era, although there were a few slightly wacky outfits among them. Some of these got rounds of applause and gasps of amazement from the audience.

Sophie heard odd comments like, "You'd never believe they weren't completely new, would you?"

For some outfits, she had been bold in her choice of colours and for one, she had put an almost transparent over-dress in vivid scarlets and oranges with a black camisole top and black velvet shorts beneath with vivid orange tights. Giant-sized beads in more bright colours hung round the neck and high black boots completed the picture. Adam's commentary made the most of each section and gained applause for each model. As they left the stage, he made an announcement.

"We're going to take a break now so you can enjoy a glass of wine and a bite to eat."

There was more applause and murmurs as people got up. In the dressing room, there was total chaos as everyone took off one outfit and put on another.

"Please," Sophie called out. "Can you hang clothes that have been worn on that rail. They'll be damaged if you just dump them everywhere. The children are coming in now for the beachwear section. We'll have the party and evening wear after that and then the wedding finale. The children will be over-excited when they get dressed in their bridesmaid clothes, so I don't want even more chaos. Thanks, everyone. It's going really well."

The interval over, the music began again and Adam started his commentary as the four little girls came on stage together, clutching buckets and spades. Their outfits emphasised the need to cover up to prevent sun damage but showed bright, trendy tops and light trousers. When the older models came on, there was once again spontaneous applause. Sophie had gone for real glamour appeal with floaty, sheer over-blouses and sequined and sparkly bikini tops.

"Definitely for showing off and not for Olympic swimming," laughed Adam. "I think I could be induced to take up sunbathing myself. Thank you, ladies."

The hair stylists were working furiously to get the next section organised. Vast amounts of hair spray were filling the air and bits of jewellery were being tucked into more formal hair arrangements for the party and evening wear. Only two of the girls were involved in the wedding finale as well as the evening section so the frenetic pace was soon slowing down.

Bee was there to help dress Phoebe and Heidi and the other two little ones. They were almost as excited as they had been at the actual wedding, but at last were dressed and stood quietly waiting for their cue.

Marnie looked beautiful in the wedding dress. "Chloe said it was a total dream and she was right. If ever I get around to getting married, I'll be booking you!"

The two partywear models came back and were quickly unzipped and transformed into bridesmaids. Sophie had toyed with the idea of modelling her own dress but decided it wasn't professional — and in any case, she wanted to walk onstage at the end in something else.

The music softened to something romantic as Adam made his introduction. "And now, our grand finale. Designed and made by Sophie, please welcome our bridal party."

The four little girls entered and walked along the catwalk two by two and holding hands. They turned with a confidence only achieved by the very young and waited as the two adult bridesmaids made their walk. The group arranged themselves across the stage and parted to let Marnie through, wearing the wedding dress itself. There were gasps from the audience and a roar of applause as Adam's sister walked slowly along the stage. The trailing bouquet was stitched in place, with the ribbons covering Rachel's damage. The whole group walked along the catwalk one more time and finally stood in a typical photographic pose along the stage.

"Ladies and gentlemen, Design by Sophie," Adam finished.

To massive applause, Sophie walked out and bowed to her applauding audience. Heidi and Phoebe came forward carrying a huge bouquet of flowers which they presented to her with beautifully timed curtseys before a smiling Adam handed her the microphone.

"Thank you all for coming. You can order anything you've seen tonight — just leave your details and we'll be in touch. I need to thank all my lovely models for giving their time so generously and to everyone backstage for their massive contribution. And special thanks to Adam, who gave me the encouragement and inspiration to launch my collection. Thank you all."

She was applauded once more as she escaped from the stage and burst into tears.

"Hey, hey. What's all this?" Adam asked. "You should be happy after such success.'

"I am. Happy, I mean. But it's been such a terrible few days and now it's all over."

"It's all just beginning, Sophie. Come on now. Wipe away those tears. We have a party to go to."

"What do you mean?"

"I've organised a party for everyone who has helped. Once the audience has gone, we're going to enjoy ourselves."

"Thank you, Adam, that's lovely, but I really must sort out some of these clothes, hang things up . . ."

"You're hopeless, woman!" he laughed. "Leave it and come and greet your guests."

Adam had organised champagne and a

delicious buffet and there was a cheer as Sophie appeared. All the models, hairdressers and make-up artists were there as well as Adam's two sisters and even his parents. Her own mother was chatting with Mrs Gilbert, looking quite relaxed.

Martha and Miles were there and congratulated her again. A number of Adam's friends and contacts who had helped came over to congratulate her and even Jemima from the television company was offering her congratulations.

In a complete whirl, Sophie spoke to as many people as she could — and remembered scarcely anything later.

In the middle of it all, Adam's phone rang. He went out of the room to answer it and came back looking shocked. He took Marnie to one side and they were deep in conversation for several minutes.

"I'm sorry Sophie, but I have to leave," Marnie said apologetically. "There's nothing for you to worry about — enjoy your evening."

"Adam? What's going on?" Sophie asked, concerned.

"It's nothing, really. Go on, talk to people and enjoy yourself."

She did as he said but kept looking back at him. He looked worried. At last, the evening was over and everyone had gone except Adam and her mother.

"I'm so proud of you, darling," her mother said, her eyes filled with tears. "And Adam, I know you've had a huge part to play in all of this. I really look forward to getting to know you better. You must come up and see our place, when Sophie eventually comes back down to earth."

"I'd like that. I'll see you in the morning, Sophie. It might not be very early, it depends on . . . look, I'll bring the van over and start loading things. If you're not here, I'll see you at your place with the first load."

She frowned when she realised that he would not be pressed. "All right, then Adam — and thank you again." He paused but merely kissed her cheek as he left.

"He's a good bloke, that one. You should snap him up while the going's good," her mother said when he'd gone.

"You're probably right. Let's go. I'm in desperate need of some sleep. It's been quite a day."

When she woke next morning, she smelled coffee and bacon and wandered through to find her mother cooking breakfast.

"Oh! You're up. I was going to bring you breakfast in bed. I'm afraid I have to get back but at least I can make sure you eat something before I go."

They sat together talking about the evening and speculating about what the future might bring. A number of people had asked for fittings for different clothes and a large number had been bought outright. It looked as if she was going to be busy for some time to come.

"It's great, isn't it, Mum?"

"It really looks as if this is it, darling. I'm sorry but I must be off now. I know you've got lots to do. Come and see us soon."

There was no sign of Adam when Sophie finally arrived at the hotel, so she began to tidy things up and was about to phone him when he arrived. He looked pale and far from his normal immaculate self.

"Come on, something's happened, I can tell. Please Adam."

"It's Rachel . . ."

"Oh, not again. What's she done this time?"

"Nothing, but she's been in a serious car accident. She was driving out of Cornwall and hit a lorry."

"Oh, my goodness. Is she all right?"

"Not really, though all things considered, not so bad. She has a broken leg and lots of scrapes and scratches but mentally, she's really flipped. She's saying things like 'Adam will have to love me now.' I think she's quite disturbed."

"Surely she can't have done it deliberately? Have you been to see her?"

"No on both counts . . . I thought if she's that obsessed, she might take it the wrong way, so Marnie spent the night at the hospital with her." Right on cue, Adam's phone rang. "This is Marnie," he said, as he answered it. "Hi. What's the news?" He listened and made a few comments and then switched the phone off, turning to Sophie.

"Rachel's sedated and had a reasonable night. They think the police will accuse her of dangerous driving but physically, she's expected to make a full recovery eventually."

"And mentally?" Sophie said anxiously.

"Marnie's persuading her to get counselling. Someone she knows who can give Rachel professional help."

"I hope so. In spite of everything, I don't wish her ill."

"That's generous of you, considering."

They worked silently, each busy with their own thoughts.

"I'll drive this lot back to the workshop and see you back here later," Adam told her.

Sophie went back inside and the hotel receptionist called her over. "There's a letter waiting for you. Someone left it at reception," she said.

Sophie opened the large, thick envelope. An untidy scrawl was underneath an impressive heading: *Gianni Medina fashions.* She drew in a sharp gasp.

Miss Gilbert, I saw your collection last night, the note read, *and I'd like to make you an offer. Please call me as soon as possible.* A flamboyant and totally illegible signature followed a mobile telephone number.

Sophie slumped into a chair. What sort of an offer? This was a large fashion house and she could hardly believe they would have found their way to Cornwall to look at an amateur little fashion show.

She carefully dialled the number with trembling fingers and gave her name.

"Sophie?" The voice had a foreign sound. "Thank you for calling. I was impressed by your show. I'm travelling back to London at the moment but I'd like to talk to you. I think I may have a place for you in my organisation. I'm always looking for new talent and I think you may be it."

"That's very flattering, thank you, but I need to think about it. I hadn't really planned to leave Cornwall. May I call you later?"

"Don't leave it for too long. I shall be returning to Paris on Sunday." She switched off and Sophie was left staring at her own phone. Could this be the big chance she had been waiting for? She heard Adam coming back.

"I forgot —" He saw her expression and asked what was wrong. Sophie showed him the letter and watched as his face fell. "Wow, congratulations. Are you taking up the offer?"

"Do you think I should?"

"If it's what you want. It is a great opportunity."

"Perhaps it is — but it's not what I want, not really. Especially not now," she said. "I'd be following orders instead of following my own creativity."

"Thank goodness you feel that way!" Adam said, obviously relieved. "But it proves you've made it, doesn't it? I always had faith in your talent, right from the start."

He smiled and added, "And of course I don't want you to go anywhere. Come here Sophie James."

He pulled her into his arms and held her close to him.

He kissed her and she kissed him back passionately, knowing at last that she was taking no risks, had nothing to fear.

"I've been so stupid. I should have trusted you," she told him. "But now I'm sure . . . I love you, Adam Gilbert. I love you now and forever."

"It's about time too," he laughed. "But you're worth waiting for, Sophie James — I knew that right from the start, too. Hang on a minute . . ."

He reached into his pocket and pulled out a length of ribbon from their earlier repairs, and he fastened it firmly around her wrist, smiling broadly.

"I'm attaching one of my strings to you, and woe betide you if you think you can ever cut it. I love you, Sophie James — and I always will. Now and forever."